"**R**osy Emmanuel Susan Lane, come in at once, your tea is getting cold," came the impatient voice of Rosy's mother from the kitchen. A wintry breeze whipped around Rosy's ankles, biting at her skin cruelly and causing her to tug her woollen socks up over her knees in frustration.

She pulled her light cardigan more tightly around her shoulders; she was determined not to let the harsh weather, or her awaiting dinner, ruin her exciting game of Cowboys and Indians.

A sudden gust of wind swept the remaining papery leaves up into the air, exposing the shimmering frosted grass beneath and whirling in front of Rosy who was balancing precariously on the raised terracotta border around her father's prized vegetable patch.

The flurry of bat-like leaves in Rosy's face caused her to lose concentration and topple right onto the bed of fruitless tomato plants, snapping some of the frozen, brittle stems. She grimaced at the flattened plants, picked herself up, and, frowning, brushed the worst of the mud off her faded pinafore.

Firing one last imaginary arrow at next-door's cat, the tall, slender nine-year-old threw down her bow and ran from the frosty November cold into the warmth of the house, sulking as her game was interrupted for the third time that afternoon. She sighed as loudly as she could, scowling in the mirror in the hallway as she passed it, noticing that her bright red 'war paint' had smudged all the way down her face.

She was rubbing at her cheek with the cuff of her tatty brown linen dress as she dashed into the kitchen, nearly knocking over the wooden chair that had been placed near the stove. Three of Mr. Lane's shirts were draped over the back of the chair, drying. Rosy pursed her lips and gently kicked the chair's leg, stubbing her toe, and proceeded to hop around on one leg clutching her foot.

Her mother turned around from the stove and cried out in shock at the state of her daughter, who looked as though she had been dragged through a hedge backwards several times. Strands of her frizzy dark brunette hair were sticking out from of her messy bob; round her head was placed a wreath of feathers, with bright blue ribbons hanging down each side of her face. Her pinafore had been torn in several places and her brown leather shoes were scuffed and dusty from the soil in the vegetable patch.

"Father Christmas will not come if he catches

you all dishevelled and dirty like this," warned Mrs. Lane wearily, sighing as she remembered that it would be Christmas Eve in a month's time. "You look like an urchin, not a sweet little girl. What on earth have you been doing *this* time?" she demanded, steadying herself on the kitchen table.

Rosy's mother was very thin and slightly frail looking, and her short, brown flyaway hair was starting to grey slightly. She always had a tired expression on her face, as would anybody who had to look after such an energetic young girl day-in day-out. Her elegantly shaped eyebrows were similar to her daughter's: thick and dark.

Even though her features were showing signs of ageing, she was still a very attractive woman with the same exotic beauty fifteen years on that her husband had first fallen for. "I'm so glad your father and I decided to stop at one child," she sighed, "what *is* that on your face?"

Rosy gave an innocent smile before replying, "I was being an Indian Squaw and I needed war paint so I used your lipstick." Before Mrs. Lane had a chance to react, the doorbell rang and, groaning, she bustled out of the room to answer it.

Rosy stood there for a few moments, then she noticed a tarnished rabbit-shaped mould lying on the table filled to the brim with glistening ruby-red jelly, its mirror-like surface gleaming in the light of the flickering oil lamp.

3

Silently, Rosy made her way towards the jelly, curious as to whether it was set yet. She cautiously prodded it with her grubby forefinger. It had not quite turned solid and her finger sunk into the wobbling dessert with a satisfying squelching sound, making Rosy giggle with delight.

At that moment her mother returned, followed by her father, who was taking off his heavy black overcoat to hang on its peg on the back of the kitchen door. He had just returned from his work at the nearby factory where his job was sorting the fruit that was to be made into jam. It was a very repetitive and tedious job and he had come home grumpy and exhausted.

"I'm sorry darling I left my keys at home again, I don't know how many times..." Mr. Lane stopped mid-sentence upon seeing Rosy standing with her finger in the jelly, covered in feathers and mud and looking sheepish. Mrs. Lane collapsed onto her husband's arm, his jaw dropping in amazement. Rosy just stood there, then ventured a meek smile.

After some stern words, Rosy had been sent to her room without any supper, and was now sitting on her bed, still with her bedraggled Indian Squaw feathers around her head. She wondered whether to creep downstairs again to retrieve her handmade wooden bow from the garden. After some time she decided to brave it, and carefully tiptoed down the stairs.

On passing the door to the sitting room, she heard her parents talking and pressed her ear to the keyhole.

"William, Rosy needs to calm down and act like a nice little girl. I made the jelly as a special treat and she made a terrible hole in the middle and it's ridiculous the amount of times I've had to make new dresses because she's ruined them all. Money is very short and I simply can't afford it."

Mr. Lane frowned and replied, "But Edith darling, we've tried everything, we are going to just have to accept the fact that she lives in her imagination, although if we could only find a way of channelling all her excess energy she would be less likely to wreak havoc in this house."

Suddenly, Rosy's mother smiled and sat up.

"I have an idea!"

Outside in the hallway, the wintry air that was leaking through the crack under the front door was starting to nip Rosy's bare skin through the thin fabric of her clothing. She tried hard to ignore how cold she was so she could listen to her parents' intriguing conversation, but to no avail. Shivering, she made her way back upstairs, annoyed at missing her mother's exciting plan.

***

After a seemingly endless wait Christmas

day had finally arrived. Rosy had woken up early in the hope that Father Christmas had placed some interesting presents in her stocking which she had hung up at the fireplace the night before. She padded barefoot across the floorboards to her parents' room and burst through the door. She was very surprised to find no one there, as she usually had to jump on them to wake them up before dragging them down to open her presents.

Baffled, she went and sat at the top of the stairs and proceeded to bump quickly down each step on her bottom, a feat that she performed every day although it gave her dreadful bruises.

After stopping at the foot of the staircase for a minute to catch her breath, she cautiously entered the living room where she found both her mother and father hurriedly placing a large parcel under the tree.

The room was filled with the festive smell of pine from the small Christmas tree which was gaily decorated with garlands of brightly coloured paper. There was already a cheery fire burning in the grate casting a warming light onto the walls and ceiling, amber coloured patterns dancing on the emerald green wall paper.

Rosy's mother had glowing and flushed cheeks as she shared a knowing smile with her equally jovial husband while trying to look inconspicuous.

Rosy grinned, curious about the mystery

present, and started towards the tree. "Open that one last!" exclaimed Mrs. Lane, unhooking the stocking from the fireplace and handing it to her daughter instead. Rosy started to rip the modest brown paper off the presents, smiling as each surprise was revealed.

So far she had acquired a book about horses from her aunt Joan, a pretty little china doll, a money box in the shape of a tiger and a painting set from her grandparents. Finally, she delved into her stocking and found an orange, which she placed on the top of her small pile of presents.

She was feeling around the bottom of the stocking to make sure that it was definitely empty when her hand brushed against something soft. Inquisitively she drew out a delicate satin rose, crimson in colour and shimmering in the flickering light of the fire. She turned enquiringly to her parents. Mrs. Lane explained,

"It's for your hair, I made it with some off-cuts." The little girl narrowed her eyes, not being the most girly child, but her mother turned her round, and swiftly combing Rosy's short chocolate coloured curls with her fingers, she slid the hair clip onto the side of Rosy's head.

Rosy moved over to the mirror on the wall and gasped, staring at the grown-up reflection smiling back at her. "Now you look like a proper young lady!" exclaimed her proud father.

"Do you like it?" asked her mother, anxiously. Rosy beamed and exclaimed,

"I love it! Thank you mother."

"Now it's time for the mysterious present under the tree!" thought Rosy. Her father handed the package to her; she was almost shaking with excitement. What could it be? It was very light and squishy as it lay on Rosy's lap, willing her to open it.

The present had been wrapped, extravagantly for the Lane household, in rustling pale pink tissue paper; a deep red ribbon had been wrapped around it, hugging it tightly and tied into a bow.

Taking a breath, Rosy pulled at the ribbon and began to remove the paper. Mr. Lane put his arm around his wife hoping that her brilliant idea would work.

As Rosy revealed a beautiful white ballet dress, her jaw dropped instantly. It had a crisp taffeta bodice and a thick fluffy skirt of snow-white netting. Underneath the dress nestled a pair of satin ballet slippers. Rosy was speechless. "But, I don't understand..." she stammered.

"Just try it on darling," smiled her mother, "go on!"

Rosy hurried to change from her flimsy nightdress into the magnificent new frock, although she was almost too scared to move for fear of ruining the pristine fabric.

Nervously, she returned to the living room where her parents beamed at their little girl.

The dress was a little too big for her, but that did not matter as she knew she would soon grow into it. "I feel like a princess!" she exclaimed.

"You look like a princess Rosy," whispered her mother. Her voice sounded choked, full of pride and relief that her plan of refining her fiery daughter was already showing signs of beginning to work!

Just putting on the dress had changed their boisterous, loud child. She had fallen quiet and was walking elegantly and with posture, as opposed to her normal rushing around like a mad thing, knocking everything over and making a racket.

Rosy knew that her parents were very poor as she only got new dresses when she ruined the old ones and she often overheard worried conversations between her parents. Her father must have worked overtime for weeks to raise enough money to buy the material.

Mr. Lane produced a small book from his pocket, and handed it to Rosy. "We can't afford to get you lessons, but there are some things in this book to get you started. Merry Christmas!"

Eagerly she rifled through the musty pages, noticing that on each one there was a beautiful illustration of a ballet step or position, every detail carefully painted with watercolour.

Rosy was speechless. She had never been good

at anything before. Suddenly she had the desire to work really hard and excel in something - could that something be ballet?

**

A few days later, Rosy came rushing home from school, a leaflet in her hand and her eyes gleaming with excitement. She slammed it down on the kitchen table and turned to her mother, who was washing up and nearly broke a plate at the sudden noise.

"Yes dear?" sighed Mrs. Lane, attempting to push the hair from her eyes with her elbow.

"A touring ballet company is coming to our area in the spring, and they'll be doing Romeo and Juliet. We're doing the play at school and I do so want to see a real ballet on the stage. Can I go?"

Rosy's mother dried her hands and came to take the leaflet from her daughter's quivering hand.

"Oh Rosy, you know we have no money. How are we supposed to buy theatre tickets?" Rosy's face fell.

"But Laura in my class said you can get them really cheap, at the back of the stalls."

"Yes, that's probably true, but even so-"

"I'll save up then, do more chores if you like."

Mrs. Lane laughed and tweaked Rosy's nose. "Good girl. I'm sure your father will give you a small pay-rise."

She would certainly make sure her husband did, as she had the feeling this production might be just the thing needed to get her plan off the ground...

Chapter Two
A NEW ADVENTURE

It had been three years since Rosy had broken or ruined anything and her mother was very pleased with herself. After the determined young girl had secured tickets to see the ballet that spring there seemed to be no subject of conversation in the Lane household that wasn't to do with dancing.

The truth was that Rosy Lane had been utterly spellbound right from curtain-up, and since then her mother had seen a change in her daughter that no one would have thought possible in such a short space of time.

Every day when she came home from school Rosy would hurry up to her bedroom, throw down her bag and put on her now considerably worn ballet shoes. Her dressing-up clothes hung forgotten in her wardrobe and, without Rosy causing chaos in the garden all the time, the neighbours were enjoying a peace and quiet they had not had for years!

There was a change in Rosy's manner too. No longer was she a distracted, high spirited child but she was in fact turning into a driven, focused young lady, who at last had found something positive to aim towards. She was walking calmly and elegantly, and she had lost a lot of puppy-fat since reading up on the dancer's diet and controlling her eating habits.

Rosy had started to live for dance. She was not only practising in her bedroom every day, but she found herself doing little feet exercises whenever she could: pliés using a kitchen chair as a barre or tiny relevés while waiting at the bus stop. She often received some funny glances from other commuters but didn't even notice.

By her twelfth birthday she had just about grown into the ballet dress and she had accomplished most of the exercises in the book even though she had not had a single lesson. She worked on her arm and leg lines until she ached all over, and every day she would practice her splits which were slowly getting better, much to her delight.

Often her mother would walk in on her and find her with her leg up the wall, grimacing and chanting, "the pain is good, the pain is good," over and over again.

It was when she grew her much-loved bobbed hair to a length with which she could achieve a ballet bun that her parents realised exactly how seriously she was taking it all. Rosy had never persevered with anything for so long before.

A few weeks after her twelfth birthday she was

up in her room as usual, getting frustrated with herself for not being able to land a pirouette neatly enough when Mrs. Lane, slightly shaken, came in and sank slowly onto the bed. "How much longer will I have to practise these stupid spins?" Rosy cried out, collapsing onto the bed next to her mother and beginning to massage her tired feet.

It was then that she noticed her mother's eyes which were red and bloodshot. "Have you been crying?" she asked, shocked to see her mother in such a state; she was normally such a strong person. "Britain has declared war on Germany," Mrs. Lane sighed, pulling her daughter towards her in a tight hug.

Rosy was confused, she didn't really understand the politics of the situation, but her mother seemed to be very distressed about it. "It'll be fine," she reassured her mother, "we still have each other." Mrs. Lane broke away from the hug and looked at Rosy, a tear rolling down her cheek onto the quilt. She took a deep breath, and grasped Rosy's hand.

"Your father has to join the army next month and... we are going to have to send you away. It's for your own safety."

Rosy closed her eyes as the room began to spin around her, wishing with all her might that she had heard wrong, that she could stay with her family that she loved so much. When she opened her eyes again she saw her mother still sitting there, frozen, staring into space, and Rosy knew that, although the idea had not quite sunk in, it was indeed the truth.

"What? I-I d-don't understand..." she stammered, looking down at her lap and gently playing with her mother's rings, deep in thought.

"All parents have been advised to evacuate their children to the country-"

"The country?" interrupted Rosy her eyes widening. She had never been out of London in her whole life, and the thought of suddenly going to live in the country was terrifying.

It was decided that Rosy should go to live with her Uncle Tom, her father's brother, up in Scotland where it was highly unlikely for her to be in danger of being bombed.

Tom had moved away from his family to live amongst nature. His first passion was painting, and he found the suburbs of London uninspiring as a subject for his work.

When his mother, Rosy's grandmother, had died, he used his inheritance to buy a large house in a tiny little village surrounded by wildlife, trees and mountains – the perfect place for an aspiring artist to live. The two brothers had not seen each other since, although when contacted he was more than happy to look after his little niece, whom he had heard so much about.

All necessary arrangements were made, and

soon it was the day before Rosy's departure. The time had come to pack her suitcase ready for her new life in the country, a task that she had been putting off for weeks. This was the hardest thing for her to do: moving all of her most precious belongings into a battered old suitcase, and knowing that she would have to leave many things behind.

Mechanically, she began taking clothing off hangers and emptying drawers, following a list that her mother had made of what to take. With each item that she added to the rest, the realisation of what was about to happen sunk in further, and Rosy's eyes filled with fresh tears that rolled down her flushed cheeks and fell onto the pile of clothes in the suitcase, creating small dark spots on the fabric.

When she had packed the essentials of underwear, socks, petticoat, handkerchiefs and blouses, there was little space left for much else. Taking the little ballet book from her bookshelf, Rosy tenderly brushed it off and placed it in the suitcase alongside a framed photograph of her smiling parents holding her as a baby.

The last thing on her list was 'mackintosh coat', which she eventually managed to squash into the suitcase with much effort.

Rosy opened her wardrobe door to check if she had forgotten anything, and there, hanging between her fairy costume and an old duffel coat, she saw her special Christmas ballet dress, gleaming as beautifully as ever.

With a cry of anguish, Rosy collapsed onto her bed; how could she have forgotten one of her most special things of all? She knew that there was no room for a single other item in her already bulging suitcase, but the dress was her pride and joy. It was the one thing that would remind her of the happy times she'd had with her family, and she could not bear to leave it at home.

"I have to take it, I simply must!" she muttered under her breath. She didn't know what it was, but something was telling her that she needed to take the dress; she had a very strange feeling that it might be important some day. A look of grim determination spread over her face.

Nervously, she removed the bulky raincoat and replaced it with the ballet dress, carefully snapping the fastenings shut and shoving the coat underneath her bed.

She sunk down onto the mattress and sighed heavily, wondering if she would get into much trouble at her Uncle's house for not bringing her coat. This lead to fresh worries about leaving her parents and the house which she so loved. She felt nowhere near ready for such an adventure.

***

"Everybody please line up here!" bellowed an intimidating and rather large uniformed lady, right next to Rosy's ear. She jumped in surprise and clung on even more tightly to her mother's hand. The station was packed with children of all ages, all standing nervously with their parents waiting for the signal to board the train which was already sitting hissing to itself at the platform.

It was a hazy September day and the sun was almost completely obscured by the dingy grey clouds that hung morosely in the sky, reflecting the mood of the families who waited for the time to come for their children to be sent to safety, away from the danger of the German bombs.

Rosy watched in silent dread as a queue of unhappy children formed and a man in some sort of official's uniform checked each one onto the train. Rosy noticed in dismay an older girl of about thirteen years comforting a small boy, her brother, who was sobbing uncontrollably, clutching a tatty-looking teddy bear in one fist and clinging on to his mother with the other.

There was a line of siblings also in the queue, steadily diminishing in size as they got younger, each with a suitcase, a gas mask and a cardboard tag hanging round their necks.

Mrs. Lane slowly produced one of these tags from her handbag, and carefully hung it round Rosy's collar, blinking back the tears as her daughter became an item of luggage, now ready to be packed onto the train that would take her to a new life at the other end of the land.

Rosy took a deep breath as her mother kissed her gently on the forehead and then stood back to let her daughter climb onto the train and disappear into the swarm of children. Each wanted to bid a last farewell to their parents and their city lives.

As Rosy joined the other evacuees in the straggling line to the door of the nearest carriage, her mother slid her shaking hand into her husband's and dabbed at her eyes with a handkerchief, joining the many other parents on the platform in saying their brave goodbyes.

Eventually, Rosy appeared at the train window, and as the engine began to move out of the station she waved as hard as she could until her mother's bright blue hat blended into the crowd and disappeared from sight.

"She will be alright won't she?" murmured her mother, shakily.

"What, our Rosy?" smiled her father. "Of course she will..!"

***

Rosy took a seat next to a group of young boys who had already started demolishing their provisions of sandwiches and apples and she

19

tearfully gazed out of the window, watching the city buildings whizz past, eventually to turn into trees and grassy fields. She felt empty inside and extremely lonely as an only child. All the other children seemed to have brothers or sisters to talk to on what her parents explained to her would be an extremely long journey.

Looking around the carriage Rosy found, with a tiny burst of pride, that she was the smartest dressed for the first time in her life. She was very proud of her new pillar-box red coat which had been bought for her especially to meet her uncle in. She had been told that first appearances were everything, and it would not be good for her to 'turn up looking like something that the cat brought in'.

She noticed an unfriendly looking girl staring over at her, keen eyes skimming over what she was wearing and carrying. Nudging her teddy bear deeper out of sight into her rucksack with her toe, Rosy averted her gaze. She wondered if the girl had noticed it and blushed slightly. Even at the age of twelve, she still had to take her teddy to bed every night in order to get to sleep, although she was very embarrassed to admit it.

The journey dragged on, and on, and Rosy began to grow tired of watching the scenery out of the window. Soon, groups of children started to leave the train to be picked up by their foster families, leaving more room in the carriage for

Rosy to stretch her legs, which were starting to cramp.

She was very disappointed that nobody had bothered to talk to her at all so far, and after shooting an icy glare at two boys who were being unnecessarily noisy she rested her head against the seat and fell asleep.

After a few more hours, Rosy awoke and she realised she was now totally alone. The carriage was completely empty, not a child in sight. She closed her eyes tightly and opened them again, thinking perhaps that she was dreaming.

When she had fallen asleep she had been surrounded by other evacuees, all tightly packed into the carriage like sardines into a tin. Now, the only objects around were a few empty paper bags which had most likely contained rations of barley sugar or dry biscuits and which now lay abandoned on the floor.

Completely isolated, sitting on the bench-seat surrounded by a tiny island of luggage, Rosy took a deep breath feeling completely deserted and more lonely than ever. "Everyone else has got off," she thought miserably to herself, "trust me to get the furthest stop in the country".

Chapter Three
IVY HOUSE

Rosy was soon placed onto a smaller train which was to take her all the way to the tiny village that would be her home. She curled up in the corner of the carriage feeling utterly miserable, then, thinking better of it, she stood up, stretching her legs for the first time in hours, and pressed her face up against the window. A tremendous sight met her eyes.

She was overlooking a vast green valley with a river meandering through the middle, which eventually reached the ocean, a sparkling blue expanse stretching endlessly out into the distance. Framing the spectacular scene were enormous mountains, partially obscured by the shimmering mist that hung in a thin layer round their peaks.

It was summer and it stayed light far into the evenings this far north. It was hard to guess the time of day, but judging by the sun, which was still high in the sky, Rosy decided that it must be mid afternoon. It was in fact six 'o clock, meaning it had been three whole hours since changing trains at Inverness.

She had gone to sleep in a large bustling town,

and now found herself speeding along the side of a mountain surrounded by rocks and valleys - and the number of trees!

Rosy had never seen so much *green* in her whole life having lived in the dusty grey streets of London for all her twelve years. For long minutes she just sat there, her eyes wide in shock, eagerly taking in every new sight.

She spent the last hour of her journey staring open mouthed out of the window, her breath misting up the glass. The excited beating of her heart was the only sound to be heard apart from the rhythmic chugging of the train.

Rosy's smile widened in wonder as she passed lochs with mirror-like surfaces and hillsides bursting with luscious green pines.

She wrestled with the latch to open the window, and when she eventually managed it a gust of fresh Highland air swept into the carriage. Immediately the smell of the pine trees hit Rosy like walking into a sweet shop on a humid day, and her smile widened even further until she thought she could smile no wider. She stuck her head right next to the open window and whooped as the refreshing air buffeted against her cheeks.

Suddenly, her hat flew clean off her head and floated quickly down into the valley below, but Rosy didn't care anymore.

As she watched the hat become a bright red

speck in the distance and finally vanish, all thoughts of missing her family and home vanished with it.

***

When Rosy arrived at the tiny village station it was eight o' clock and still quite light. The place was deserted, not a soul in sight. She waved goodbye to the train driver, a cheery man with a thick white moustache, and then after carefully putting her suitcase on the ground, she wondered what to do.

She looked around her at her picture-postcard surroundings. There was a tiny waiting room which looked really pretty. It seemed like something straight out of a fairytale book with its white weather-boarded exterior and bottle-green painted window frames.

The benches and lampposts on the platform were painted in the same jolly shade and there was an old rusty cart sitting in the middle of the platform, on which stood several milk churns waiting to be delivered.

It had obviously just been raining as large puddles lay on the platform, and each bench was covered in tiny water droplets, which glistened on the freshly painted surfaces. Rosy did not want to sit on them, get wet and turn up at her new home looking worse than she inevitably did already, so with a sigh she sat on the dry leather of her suitcase, and waited. After what seemed like hours, there was still no sign of her uncle, or any human being for that matter. Rosy started to feel extremely anxious.

It was beginning to get dark and she did not like the idea of being alone in this strangely quiet place any longer. She was so used to the bustling city, and the comfort of always having someone around; surely her uncle had not forgotten about her?

Even though it was summer and the air was quite humid she began to shiver, and every noise in the otherwise silent atmosphere sent a feeling like cold fingers creeping all the way down her spine, which she did not like at all.

She had just started to enjoy her adventure, but now, sitting timidly on her own in an unfamiliar place, her previous excitement was beginning to turn into homesickness and fear.

Just when she was about to burst into tears, Rosy heard a distant noise which she recognised immediately. It was a motor car's engine! The car got nearer and nearer until eventually the station echoed with the sound as it turned the last corner.

Relief flooded over Rosy as she saw a very short, old woman get out and head towards her, walking surprisingly quickly but with a very slight limp, her back arched over a wooden walking stick.

"Rosy Lane?" the woman asked in a very

distinct Highland accent, reaching out to help her up from the suitcase. She had a soft, friendly-sounding voice, and Rosy began to like her straight away. Nodding shyly, Rosy took the woman's hand, which was as soft as her voice, and picked up her luggage.

The only car that Rosy had ever been in was a taxi in the city, and that definitely wasn't as grand as the one that she was getting into now. It had shining black paintwork, elegant metal spokes on the wheels and comfortable-looking burgundy leather seats.

"Is this your car?" she asked, fascinated, as the old woman helped her into the passenger seat.

"Oh no!" she replied cheerfully, "this is your uncle Tom's. I'm Mrs. McGregor, his housekeeper. I only learnt to drive because I used to help out with the tractors on a farm."

"Uncle Tom has a motor car!" exclaimed Rosy excitedly, grinning at Mrs. McGregor even more. Her parents would never have been able to afford anything so expensive or luxurious, especially now the war was on.

Rosy spent the short journey to her new house marvelling at the crumbling stone cottages and fields of heather they were driving alongside, her mouth constantly open in wonderment.

Although it was not so light now, Rosy could see Mrs. McGregor clearly as she concentrated on negotiating the hairpin bends that led into the village. She must have been at least seventy years old, as her face was lined with wrinkles, reminding Rosy of the streams that networked vein-like down the sides of the mountains.

Her eyes were bright and youthful, with creases spreading out from the corners when she smiled, which was often. Her thin grey hair was scraped back into an old-fashioned knot at her neck beneath a smart navy blue hat, which matched her woollen coat.

After about twenty minutes they turned off the main road up a small hill shrouded with dense woodland, and passed what looked like a large wooden sign with some writing on it, which Rosy could not read in the darkness. Eventually they arrived at a house, and Mrs. McGregor turned off the engine.

Rosy could not believe her eyes! Before her stood a very pretty house, lit up by the headlights of the car. It was neat and symmetrical, with an unusually wide front door and nine large square windows. The picturesque stone exterior was overgrown with a thick layer of ivy, spreading over a few of the windows and up onto the roof.

"This," pronounced the housekeeper proudly, "is Ivy House." Rosy just smiled to herself quietly, before taking Mrs. McGregor's hand and jumping out of the car. The old lady opened the gleaming red door and ushered Rosy inside. Immediately, the warmth hit her, she had forgotten that she was actually quite cold.

Looking around, Rosy noticed that they were in a small entrance hall with a cold stone floor and numerous brass hooks on the wall, which overflowed with all manner of coats and jackets. Opposite the front door and slightly to the left was a magnificent carpeted staircase and, on the walls, there were several paintings of the surrounding countryside, presumably by her uncle himself. The general atmosphere was cosy and welcoming, and Rosy soon began to feel at home.

"Thomas!" shouted Mrs. McGregor, taking off her coat and hanging it on top of a worn green raincoat on the nearest peg. Rosy experienced another pang of guilt as she remembered that her mackintosh was still underneath her bed, hundreds of miles away in London.

She wondered how long it would be until she received an angry letter from home but tried to push that thought to the back of her mind. After all, she had more important things to think about right now. A flutter of nerves returned to her as she prepared to meet her new family and her grip tightened on the handle of her suitcase.

"Tom!" Mrs. McGregor repeated, sighing, "This child has been travelling for hours to meet you, you could at least *be* here to welcome her." On the word 'be' she slammed her walking stick down hard on the stone floor. The resulting crack echoed around the spacious house eerily, and Rosy nearly jumped out of her skin in surprise. "Sorry dear," she apologised, "but honestly, your uncle really needs to-"

Her speech was cut off by a shout of, "Sorry Effie, I'm coming," and shortly afterwards hurried footsteps approached from upstairs.

"Effie?" Rosy questioned, with a puzzled look at Mrs. McGregor.

"Euphemia," she explained, her eyes sparkling, "it's my name, dreadful isn't it?"

"Oh no, I think it's a beautiful name!" protested Rosy, whereupon the old woman took her hand and smiled,

"I think we are going to get on just fine."

"Hello Rosy!" came a voice from the staircase. Tom Lane was a very handsome, very tall man of about thirty five years old. He ran down the stairs two at a time, buttoning up his smart white shirt with one hand and smoothing back his untamed mop of curly brown hair with the other.

He was smiling jovially, as if receiving a twelve year old niece into his home was a daily occurrence. Rosy was mildly surprised that he didn't have a Scottish accent, before realising that he had lived in London, like her, for the majority of his life.

"Come through," he offered, placing her luggage by the staircase and guiding her through to what seemed to be a living room where there was a comforting fire burning in the grate.

In this room there was a whole wall dedicated to books, mostly on art, and several squashy armchairs, onto which Rosy wanted nothing more than to just collapse in relief.

During such a long journey to get to Ivy House, she had had ample time to think about what her life would be like in a completely unfamiliar world, who she would meet, whether she would be happy. She liked her uncle very much already, and his housekeeper Mrs. McGregor had been so kind.

Rosy looked around the room in amazement, taking in the piles and piles of paperwork and books and unfinished cups of tea. Tom was evidently not very organised. The comfy chairs were all covered in fabrics of different colours, patterns and styles, which clashed terribly, but in a way made the room so much more endearing. It was obvious that this room belonged to a single man.

Gesturing to the chair opposite him, Tom sat down and crossed his legs very informally. Rosy stifled a giggle; her father would never have been so casual around her. But after all, her uncle was not an ordinary man. Rosy had already decided this fact by judgement of his unusual taste in upholstery.

Chapter Four
THE LOCKET

When Rosy woke up the next morning she found herself still in her travelling clothes. She was lying snugly wrapped up in a thick multicoloured patchwork quilt which was beautifully soft and had a satisfying soapy smell.

She was on a narrow bed with an ornately carved wooden board at her feet, and the mattress she was lying on was spongy and far more comfortable than her bed at home. She propped herself up on her elbows, then groggily swung her feet out of bed and sat up, rubbing her eyes and letting out a tremendous yawn.

Trying to ignore the dizzy, lightheaded feeling that always comes with standing up too quickly, she rose to her feet, and promptly sunk back down again trying to remember where she was. With a mixture of nervousness and incredible excitement she remembered everything: Mrs. McGregor the charming and very Scottish housekeeper, her Uncle Tom, relaxed and carefree, and her new home, which she was looking forward to exploring!

The room she was in was clean and bright with enormous dormer windows from which were streaming rays of sunlight, creating puddles like molten gold on the bare wooden floorboards. Rosy sat for a minute watching the tiny particles of dust that were dancing in the light and then had a second go at getting out of bed.

This time she succeeded, and she walked around the room for a while taking everything in. There was a wardrobe, a large chest of drawers and a dressing table with beautifully carved birds and flowers at the top of each leg.

Next to the bed was a wash basin, where was stood a jug of water and a bowl for washing, and the dusty floorboards were partially covered in the centre of the room by a worn, elegantly patterned rug with tassels at each end.

All of the walls were painted a brilliant white, making the room seem even larger than it was, and the streams of light that came in through the windows reflected around the room giving an appearance of airy spaciousness.

One of the walls was steeply sloping, so Rosy guessed that the room must be at the very top of the house, in the attic. With a contented smile, she did a few quick pirouettes and discovered with relief that there was ample space for dancing.

She was cavorting around the room when there came a muffled knock, and Mrs. McGregor popped her head around the door. She was dressed in a shocking tartan dressing gown with matching carpet slippers and she smiled when she saw Rosy up and awake already. "Your breakfast is served!" she said, gesturing behind her down the stairs.

A delicious smell of bacon and eggs was wafting up the staircase from somewhere below, making Rosy's mouth water. She realised that she had not eaten since her sandwiches on the train the day before and that was many hours to go without food for a twelve year old!

Following her out of the room, Rosy made her way down three flights of winding staircases, different from the one that she saw leading off from the front hall. As if she had heard her thoughts, Mrs. McGregor broke the silence. "This was the servants' staircase a long time ago," she informed Rosy with a knowing wink, "but now it is your own personal right of way. It leads straight from the door of your bedroom to the kitchen."

Just as she finished her sentence, she opened the door at the bottom of the staircase and found the source of the wonderful breakfasty smell. They had emerged into a small kitchen where Tom was already sitting at the table reading a newspaper. On top of the bright red enamelled stove was a huge pan of fried eggs, and eight rashers of bacon lay sizzling quietly in a frying pan.

The kitchen was fitted out with wooden cupboards, and each door had a different coloured handle. Each chair also was painted in a different merry shade; Rosy felt as if she had stepped into a rainbow. How different this jolly room was from her drab kitchen at home. She wondered if all kitchens were like this in the country.

Upon hearing the door creak open, Tom looked up from his paper and his face split into a warm smile when he saw Rosy lurking hungrily in the doorway. "Come and sit down!" he invited, pulling a bright orange chair out from underneath the table. Rosy sat down rather timidly, as it still felt strange to her to be in someone else's house, someone else's world.

"Is breakfast ready yet Effie?" he asked, folding up his newspaper carefully and then flinging it to one side. It landed in a crumpled heap on the floor.

"Nearly," came the ever-patient reply. As Mrs. McGregor bustled round the kitchen preparing the breakfast, Tom had a chance to get to know his unusual-looking little evacuee.

"So, how was the journey?" he asked, grinning as a huge plate of breakfast was placed before him. There was a mountain of steaming bacon surrounded by a moat of glistening baked beans and mushrooms, and on top of all this lay a large white fried egg with a rich yellow yolk.

Breakfast at home for Rosy consisted of toast with a watery poached egg and occasionally a few slices of thin bacon, which was usually as tough as boot leather and tasted like it too.

As Rosy tucked in to this welcome feast with wide eyes, she told her uncle all about her long and tiring expedition from London. "Nobody talked to me at all!" she exclaimed between mouthfuls of mushroom and toast. "They all seemed so unfriendly."

"I don't think you will have any trouble with that here," said Tom.

Rosy smiled thankfully. She had been worrying about how she would be welcomed for days, and being ignored on the train had made her really quite upset. However, if everybody in this village was as nice as Tom and Mrs. McGregor, she knew that she had nothing to worry about at all.

**

Ten minutes later, when all the breakfast things had been cleared away, Tom declared that the new arrival should be taken on a tour of the village, at which point Rosy's face fell. She was worried about meeting so many new people dressed as she was in her shabby, worn clothes.

She told her fears out loud, but all the reassurance she got was a mysterious instruction to go back to her room and explore all the furniture, open each door and drawer, and be back down again, smartly dressed, in half an hour's time. Rosy sprinted up the poky staircase right to the top of the house and entered back into her room.

She crossed the floorboards to get to the wardrobe and, apprehensively, she opened the door, gasping in delight as she saw four dresses each of a different colour, hanging there new and pristine. She opened the drawer at the bottom and found three shiny pairs of shoes, one black pair, one brown pair and one white pair. Everything was in her size; her mother must have written and given uncle Tom her measurements.

Rosy seldom got new clothes or shoes at home, her parents were far too poor, so this was even better than Christmas! She had never realised exactly how well-off her uncle was. She ran around the room like a mad thing, opening drawers and discovering new things each time. There were new blouses and skirts, petticoats and socks and ribbons for her hair.

In the last drawer she opened she found a small black box and next to it a piece of paper with some writing on. She gingerly took the lid off the box and there, sparkling in the sunlight, was a small locket which hung on a thin silver chain.

Rosy opened the locket with trembling hands and found that tiny pictures had been placed in both windows. The first was a recent photograph of her with her mother and father, and the second one of Rosy herself, clutching her new ballet shoes and beaming from ear to ear. Next she read the note which had been written by her mother.

"My Dearest Rosy, I hope that you arrived at your uncle's house alright and are settling in well. I told him of your concern for appearances and he kindly offered to set you up with some new clothes. He says that his housekeeper made the dresses herself.

"The locket is from your father and me, it was your grandmother's – look after it won't you? Your father has been sent away to fight but I am sure he will be perfectly fine. I am well, although I am missing you terribly already. Make sure that you write every week to tell me how you are getting on! All of my love always – Mother".

On reading this letter in her mother's familiar scrawly handwriting, twinges of homesickness set in and she blinked rapidly to keep back the tears. Putting on a confident face, she reminded herself that she was twelve now. She had to be brave and put such thoughts behind her, and as soon as she returned to the wardrobe to choose a dress to wear, her worries vanished almost completely.

Finding it hard to contain her excitement, she rifled through the curtain of pretty fabrics and finally picked out a pale blue dress with pleats at the front of the skirt. It had elbow-length sleeves and a leather belt to fasten at the waist. It would make Rosy look very grown up and sophisticated. Her old brown pinafore and dull beige blouse lay discarded on the floor as she slipped into a fresh petticoat.

The cool, sleek fabric felt soft against her skin, and as she continued to dress she felt like a new person. After pulling on a pair of lacy white ankle socks, she took the brown pair of shoes from the drawer, stroking the smooth leather lovingly. They had a modest heel and a strap with a buckle, and Rosy spent the next few minutes parading round the room admiring them.

Very soon after, Rosy drew her thick, frizzy hair into two neat plaits and tied them with matching blue ribbons, then finally, she placed the gleaming silver locket around her neck. She twirled in front of the mirror, very pleased with what she saw. The colour of the dress made her eyes stand out against her snowy pale skin; she had never realised how blue they were before.

Making her way back down to the kitchen, she found Tom helping his housekeeper with the washing up. As the door creaked open, they looked up and smiled at the considerably smarter Rosy who was standing bashfully before them. "There," exclaimed Mrs. McGregor, "now isn't that an improvement?"

Overwhelmed with gratitude, Rosy rushed to hug the old lady and her uncle in turn, still in disbelief at her good luck to be surrounded by such kindly people. "I don't know what to say!" she murmured, shaking her head in astonishment.

"I'm just so glad that you take such a pride in your appearance," beamed Mrs. McGregor affectionately, "I've heard of so many evacuees from London who are riddled with lice and other such things..."

She was interrupted by Tom, who took Rosy by the hand, his rich brown eyes sparkling. "I think it is time for you to explore your new village!"

Chapter Five
A MATCHING MARIGOLD

As Rosy skipped excitedly away from Ivy House, Tom picked something off of a plant that grew parallel to the gravel path and presented it to his neice. It was a delicate marigold flower with petals of a brillant orange colour. Rosy smiled radiantly and tucked it into her belt, happily placing her hand into his.

Immediately in front of Ivy House was the start of a dusty track. It led through the middle of a large field which was rather peculiar as dotted around were pitched dozens of tents. Families were milling about, adults cooking breakfast over small fires while children played games on the grass.

"What?-" started Rosy, turning to face Tom, now completely baffled.

"This is 'Ivy House Camping Site', favourite holiday place for many British families!" he announced proudly, waving to a group of people who were hanging out their washing on a rickety make-shift washing line.

"I found that just being an artist didn't make me a sufficient living, so I bought up the land that surrounded my house and turned it into a campsite!

People still come up to escape from the war-worries that dominate city life. In the winter I offer bed and breakfast in the house." Rosy was impressed.

"You set all of this up on your own?" she gasped, jumping nimbly over a pothole in the road and managing not to scuff her new shoes. The days of the careless, scruffy Rosy had disappeared since she had discovered dancing, a passion which had turned her into a far more refined young lady.

She decided that living on a campsite would be tremendous fun as there would be lots of other children to play with all the time. Rosy would have liked to stay there a bit longer and get to know a few of the campers, but there was a lot more to see and do in the village so Tom gently dragged her away and started off towards the far end of the field.

They walked along the track until they came to an old rusty gate which instead of opening they just climbed over. On the other side was the wooden sign that Rosy had noticed the night before when Mrs. McGregor had driven her from the station.

She could now clearly read the writing, which gave the name of the campsite in neat painted lettering. It also said 'Owner - Mr. Thomas Lane', and Rosy felt a squirm of pride to see her family name written there.

Tom wanted to show Rosy the beach first, so he lead her down the hill, which was shaded from the hot summer sun by a canopy of leafy green trees, and lead straight down to the sea. On the left stood a tiny Post Office building with crates outside the door. They were piled up high with mountains of soily vegetables. An elderly woman in a straw hat, presumably the shop's owner, was helping a small boy pile carrots into a huge basket.

"Everybody who does not grow their own food gets it from the Post Office which doubles up as a village store," Tom told her, cheerily waving to a passer-by. He seemed to know everyone they passed in the street, or if they weren't acquainted they always greeted each other politely with a friendly smile.

"What's that wooden building next to it?" asked Rosy.

"That *was* the old Post Office and the shop's storeroom. It's never used now, I don't know what they're going to do with it. Pull it down I expect. Shame, it's got charm."

Next to that was a row of neat little houses each with cheerfully painted window frames and front doors. Occasionally a small horse-drawn cart would clatter past, its passengers waving to Rosy in welcome. They crossed the road and descended the steep bank onto the beach.

The view was spectacular. An azure-blue bay stretched out on both sides as far as the eye could see, where it met the misty silhouettes of the mountain peaks many miles away. The small amount of sky that could be seen through the dense wispy layers of cotton wool cloud was a dazzling sapphire colour.

The bitter tang of sea air and seaweed lingered thickly in the air and caught in the back of Rosy's throat making her cough. Just then a sheep bolted from the trees and came running clumsily across the beach, its hooves crunching noisily on the broken shells and pieces of coral which were mixed in with the sand.

Rosy screamed in terror, and darted behind her uncle, clinging tightly to his jacket, her heart beating fast. "What was that?" she cried, emerging cautiously, still clutching Tom's arm.

"That was a sheep Rosy, you are going to have to get used to them, they are everywhere in Scotland."

Rosy was shaken. She had never seen a sheep before in her life, and you can imagine how terrifying it would be to come across one for the first time. It had devilish horns and shadowy black eyes, and had made such a terrific noise as it galloped madly past. "I'm sorry uncle," she began but was interrupted,

"No, please call me Tom!"

She nodded and carried on. "I made such a fuss, you must think that I am awfully silly." Tom knelt down to his niece's height.

"Rosy, I understand. Of course you are going to

be afraid of these animals. I mean, you have never come across any apart from dogs and cats in your life!" Rosy smiled and nodded again. "We need to introduce you to some more wildlife," he decided, starting to walk down the beach towards a cluster of stone buildings in the distance.

"That is 'Allaway Farm'" he told her, "I have never actually been there in the five years I've been living in the village, but we can go and take a look if you like." Rosy nodded eagerly as she had only ever seen a farm in children's books, and they did look lovely.

As they walked away from the neat and well-kept main street, the terrain became rockier and wilder. The road became uneven and the undergrowth seemed to be more dense and untamed compared to the cultivated trees of the central village.

They neared the farm, and Rosy noticed that it was complete with farmhouse, pond and a wide wooden gate, behind which many large white geese could be seen, waddling around and honking lustily.

"Ah," uttered Tom, stopping at the gate nervously and jumping back as a slender feathered neck poked through the bars and snapped playfully at his ankles. "Now, geese," he said, "I'm with you there, terrified of them!" Rosy started to giggle, and, although he was slightly embarassed, Tom joined in too.

They were cut short in their laughter by a friendly shout from the door of the farm house.

"Hello! Can I help you?" The voice was from a young girl of about Rosy's age with a stunning mass of white-blonde hair which hung straight as a poker around her waist. She was wearing a shirt and fawn coloured jodhpurs with knee-high black riding boots and she looked very smart. She ran straight through the gaggle of geese towards them, a smile splitting across her face as she approached Rosy and her uncle.

"You're the new evacuee, aren't you?" she grinned, holding out her hand which was covered in mud from helping out with the horses.

"That's right," Rosy replied, shaking it and not minding the dirt at all. She liked this cheery girl a lot already. Her new friend introduced herself as Audrey Price, the farmer's daughter, and offered to take Rosy and Tom around the farm.

They accepted gladly and they climbed the fence, Tom still wary of the geese which were happily flapping about the yard around their feet. They visited the cows, pigs and sheep, followed in their progress by Audrey's border collie dog. Rosy's confidence around the animals gradually increased with Audrey's reassurance.

Lastly, they came to the horses which were all in a field at the back of the buildings, munching lazily at the luscious green grass. As they approached, a beautiful silver-grey mare came trotting up to the fence, and Rosy reached out a tentative hand to touch its face. She tenderly stroked the animal's glossy coat and soft velvety nose, smiling as the horse breathed tickly warm air onto her hand and whinnied gently.

"Her name is Nessie, after the Loch Ness Monster," explained Audrey, scrunching up her brow in thought, "I'm not sure why. She likes you though!"

Rosy beamed and tucked her hand into Nessie's thick silver mane. She felt all funny inside, but it was a nice feeling, one that she had only ever felt before when dancing. She had never been so close to a horse before, and she really liked it. Nessie was so warm and friendly and soft to touch.

Audrey looked on with interest, excited at the prospect of having introduced someone to the wonder of animals. "My father has gone to Inverness to buy some more animal feed and my big sister Eve is out on a hack with some pupils from the riding school, but we could have some drinks if you want," Audrey said eventually. Tom said they could stay, which pleased the girls immensely.

"What's a hack?" asked Rosy, following Audrey towards the farmhouse, where there was a picnic table in the garden.

"You ride on a trail around the countryside. I absolutely love them, they're so much fun, especially on a lovely day like this." Audrey kicked aside a bucket which was in the middle of the path, and continued. "Eve is a riding instructor!" she announced, obviously very proud of her sister. "If you sit down here, I'll go in and get changed."

Rosy and Tom settled down and enjoyed the peace of the colourful garden, watching the busy bees buzzing to and fro as they explored the abundant flower beds. Ten minutes later Audrey reappeared, now fresh and clean in a sunny marigold frock with white lace around the neck and sleeves.

"I love your dress," exclaimed Rosy, suddenly having an idea. Getting up, she took the flower from her belt, and tucked it into Audrey's hair, where it stayed, matching the fabric of her dress perfectly.

The two girls grinned at each other, and Audrey took her new friend's hand in delight. "Come and help me with the drinks!"

***

Tom, Rosy and Audrey spent a blissful morning at the farm sipping sweet homemade lemonade and chatting about everything. "Why is the farm called Allaway?" asked Tom, and Audrey explained,

"I'm not sure but it comes from the Scottish words meaning 'wild field'. I suppose it is pretty wild around here!" Audrey beamed radiantly, something which she did a lot, and her smile was infectious. She seemed to be such a happy person, and one couldn't help but like her.

They discovered that Rosy would be in the same class at school as Audrey, although there were only two classes in total. There were so few children in the village that it was needless to have any more teachers.

The summer holidays would end in two weeks time, and it was decided that Audrey would meet Rosy at the campsite on the first day of term as her route to the school went past it, and they would walk together.

"We must meet up tomorrow Rosy," said Audrey, draining her glass of lemonade and sticking her finger in to scoop out the bits.

"Definitely," Rosy replied, "that will be brilliant!" Tom glanced at his watch, and jumped up in alarm.

"It's twelve o'clock already, goodness, where has the time gone? We really must go Rosy, Effie always makes lunch for half past."

Sadly, Rosy waved goodbye to her new friend and followed her uncle back down the uneven road that wound alongside the beach. Tom was overjoyed that his niece had made such a nice friend already.

The walk back was quite long, and they were

only halfway back to the house when the heavens opened and it began to pour with rain.

They had been too busy talking to notice that the perfect blue sky and pure white clouds had turned to an ominous grey, and the sudden downpour caught them unawares. "Oh!" cried Rosy in despair, as her beautiful dress quickly became saturated with warm, but nevertheless still very wet water.

They ran the rest of the way home and arrived on the doorstep of Ivy House gasping and bedraggled. Tom fumbled in his sodden pockets for his keys, finally finding them and ushering Rosy in before him. They were met in the hallway by an annoyed Mrs. McGregor who reminded them that they were ten minutes late for their lunch.

"We are sorry Effie," panted Tom, meekly, peeling off his limp jacket and hanging it on the doorhandle to dry out, "it was so warm and sunny when we left." Mrs. McGregor sighed.

"How long have you lived in Scotland? Five years? And you still haven't learnt that the weather is unpredictable!"

She suggested that they go and stand by the stove in the kitchen to dry off, and followed them down the hallway.

"Now, I think we should put Rosy's raincoat on a peg in the hall. Where is it dear? I'll go and get it for you." Rosy froze and swallowed nervously.

"I haven't got it," she murmered almost silently.

"Sorry? I didn't hear." This was it. Rosy took a deep breath and told herself to be brave.

"I left it at home," she said, louder this time.

Mrs. McGregor frowned, her face becoming stern. "It was on your list wasn't it?"

"Yes, it was," replied Rosy, starting to cry. "I'm sorry, but I needed to bring my ballet things, and the raincoat wouldn't fit in. And now I've ruined my beautiful new dress that you've been so kind to make for me, and you're going to be really angry with me, and..."

Tom interrupted, "Shhh now, Effie isn't angry, just surprised." The housekeeper's angry expression softened slightly,

"Yes," she said, "I just thought that you were a sensible young lady!" Rosy sniffed,

"Oh, but I am, I am, I just couldn't leave my lovely ballet dress at home, my mother made it even though she is so poor, and it would..." she collapsed into another fit of sobs that would make even the stoniest of hearts melt.

"You never told me about your dancing. It must mean a great deal to you," said Tom. Rosy composed herself and began to tell them everything, from that first Christmas when she had received the ballet dress, shoes and book, to her parents being too poor to get her lessons.

"I practice exercises from the book almost every day. I can be somebody else for that short time. I forget all of my worries when I am dancing."

Mrs. McGregor forgot to be angry. "The dress isn't ruined my dear," she reassured the sniffling Rosy. "It'll dry. Dear me, this is a commotion. I'll write to your mother and ask her to send the coat, but in the meantime let's sit down and eat some lunch." Rosy dried her eyes thankfully and tucked into the plate of jam sandwiches that was placed in front of her.

The jam was gloopy and deliciously sweet with scrumptious lumps of real strawberries nestling in it. "This is Effie's own jam, she makes it herself," said Tom, taking a bite out of his sandwich and watching the jam ooze thickly out of the side. As they sat in silence enjoying the lunch, Tom's brain was working hard.

Rosy obviously loved her dancing more than anything and he so wanted her to be happy while she was staying with him. "Rosy," he ventured with a hopeful grin. "How would you like it if I got you ballet lessons?" His eyes twinkled as Rosy's face lit up and she smiled more that she had ever smiled before. She stood up and threw her arms around his neck.

"Oh, thank you Tom, I should think I'm the luckiest person in the world!"

Chapter Six
BALLET CLASS

Over the two remaining weeks of the school holidays, when she wasn't helping out at the campsite, Rosy spent all her free time with Audrey and the two became inseparable. The sight of the blonde straight haired Audrey Price with the new dark frizzy-haired evacuee girl became familiar to the villagers. The two were always on the beach with Audrey's dog, paddling in the refreshing blue water or just strolling and chatting.

When Rosy told her that she was to start ballet lessons in the village, Audrey let out a shriek of delight as she, too, attended at the same time every week!

She spent a whole afternoon enlightening her curious friend with everything she needed to know about the teacher, Madame Odette, and exactly what went on in each lesson, until Rosy became absolutely wild with excitement and had to sit down to catch her breath.

As luck would have it, the uniform for the dancing school was a white tarlatan frock, and, upon receiving Rosy's first letter home, her mother was overjoyed to find out that her handiwork had come to some real use at last. Audrey taught Rosy how to tie her hair in a proper ballet bun, then started to teach her some of the exercises she would need for class.

When the day came for Rosy's first lesson there was no gleaming sun streaming through the windows to wake her up in the morning, so when Mrs. McGregor poked her head around the door to check that she was up, Rosy was still wrapped tightly in her quilt, fast asleep. When Effie woke her, she jumped to her feet at once, throwing on the first blouse and skirt she came to, though not forgetting to put on her silver locket.

She was half an hour behind her intended schedule, and not wanting to hurry her breakfast and cause indigestion later on, she simply skipped it. For one final time she checked through her ballet bag, in which were her prized white dress, shoes, socks and hairpins. Then, waving goodbye to Tom and Mrs. McGregor, she dashed out of the front door into the dull morning.

Thankfully, she arrived on time at the village hall where the classes were held. Audrey was waiting for her by the front gate. Grabbing her hand breathlessly, she led Rosy through to a big room with benches and coat pegs lining the walls, where there were already a few young girls getting changed into their uniforms.

Slightly nervously Rosy began to do the same,

and when she had finished, Audrey helped her to put up her hair in a tidy bun at the base of her neck. The few stubborn curls at the sides of her face were kept from falling into her eyes by a thick white ribbon.

Standing there surrounded by new faces and in a completely strange uniform, Rosy felt really out of place, but as soon as she slipped her familiar satin ballet shoes onto her feet she felt much better.

Tying the ribbons tightly around her ankles with practised ease she glanced up at Audrey, who was warming up her feet by massaging them vigorously. Noticing Rosy looking apprehensively up at her, Audrey gave her a friendly hug, and pulled her to her feet. "You have absolutely nothing to worry about," she reassured her, "Madame Odette may come across slightly scary but she's lovely really! You'll enjoy yourself, promise."

Feeling better, Rosy smiled boldly even though her stomach was doing flips inside her. She was really scared of doing something wrong and looking like a fool, but, she reminded herself sternly, she couldn't be expected to know everything. This was, after all, her first ever ballet lesson. Linking arms with an elated Audrey, they followed their fellow pupils into the hall.

The room had a very high ceiling, which made it seem much bigger than it actually was. There were flimsy net curtains over each of the windows to shield them from the view of passers-by and at one end of the hall there was a large stage with rich burgundy curtains that hung in heavy pleats at each side.

The parquet floor had been polished so that it had a shining mirror-like surface underfoot, and in the corner of the space stood an ancient piano. Here sat a very tall, bald, cheery man who was hastily finishing his breakfast of bread and an apple while simultaneously sorting out his music for the lesson.

Standing next to the piano was an attractive middle-aged woman in a long flowing skirt and leotard; both of them were chuckling away to something that the man had just said. The woman was Madame Odette, an ex-principal-ballerina who had met her Scottish husband while performing in a touring production.

She moved to the Highlands with him not long afterwards when her professional career was nearing its end, but found she could not leave her dancing life behind her. So she set up a tiny dancing school to cater for the handful of village children, and had loved every minute of her teaching career since.

When she noticed the children emerging from the dressing room, she straightened up, still giggling quietly to herself, and crossed over to the front of the room. "Ah! 'Ello, welcome Rosy," she addressed her new pupil in a clipped French accent with heavily rolled 'r's, which was rather intimidating until you got used to it.

Rosy curtsied shyly, much to the delight of the teacher who was rather old fashioned in her ways and warmed straight away to this polite, somewhat exotic-looking girl.

Rosy had unusually dark hair and thick, striking eyebrows, and reminded Odette very much of herself when she was young. With a friendly smile, she ushered Rosy to a place at the front of the class next to Audrey and began the lesson.

As her first ballet class went on, Rosy was enjoying every minute of it. Madame Odette reminded her of a sergeant major who conducted the exercises in an almost military style, allowing the girls to have fun but knowing when to be strict and making them work until they ached all over. She kept her expert eye on Rosy throughout the lesson and was very impressed by her already extensive knowledge of the steps.

Occasionally, if Madame Odette made everyone repeat an exercise over and over again until perfect, the pianist, whom Rosy later learnt was called Alistair, would change the traditional music halfway and start playing a jolly music hall number with a swinging bass line.

This made the unsuspecting teacher break out into another fit of raucous laughter which rang round the building and was so loud that it at first caused Rosy to lose her concentration and get the steps muddled up.

"Now can we 'ave posé turns ladies?" requested Madame Odette. "Groups of four please. Rosy, you 'aven't done these before 'ave you? Oh well, just follow everyone else and you will be fine." Everyone huddled into the corner of the room and Alistair began to play the delicate melody of Für Elise as the first group span unsteadily across the room.

Alistair's beautiful accompaniment eventually became drowned out by shouts of "Spot, SPOT ladies! Find a spot on the wall and glue your eyes to it!" and "Concentrate Mary, 'ave you not been listening? Toe to the knee - where is your knee?"

Rosy found herself in a group with Audrey and the identical Morrison twins who had fiery orange hair and fiery eyes to match. Madame Odette had ordered them to wear different colour hair ribbons to class after growing annoyed with the confusion of shouting at the wrong twin during exercises. Edine wore a green ribbon and Faye a violet one.

They smiled encouragingly at Rosy as their turn neared, and eventually came the cry of "Audrey's group! – une, deux, trois, *and*!"

Because they were the last four to follow the diagonal line of posé turns across the hall, the others were standing at the other side, watching, having finished their turns. Rosy's stomach lurched as she felt everyone's eyes on her, summing up the 'new girl'. The floor suddenly looked even more slippery than before.

She set her mind on the task and launched herself towards the opposite corner, which also now looked further away. She performed several perfectly executed spins, but then lost her balance, knocked into an equally unstable Edine and fell, hard, onto the floor. There were a few giggles from the other girls and Rosy blushed a deep crimson as she carefully picked herself up and brushed the dust off her tutu.

She was mortified. She had fallen over in front of everyone in her first lesson, and she must have looked really stupid. Seeing her distraught face, Madame Odette rushed over and placed a gentle hand on Rosy's shoulder.

"Falling over is nothing to be ashamed of Rosy, in fact, why did nobody else do it? It means that you were not afraid to take risks!" She chortled wickedly and clapped her hands together before saying, "Pirouettes ladies! And I want everyone to 'ave fallen over by the end, but do try to get up again in time for the last chord. Last one standing is the winner!"

Alistair thumped out 'Knees up Mother Brown' with great vigour and the girls began the pirouette exercise – "Echapé, relevé, spin and *double*!" Rosy was the only one who could manage a double pirouette with relative ease, and soon, after Audrey had almost managed one but then lost balance and slipped to the floor, Rosy was the only one left standing, with the rest of the class reduced to a giggling mess.

When they realised that Rosy had won, and was still performing the exercise with a triumphant look on her face, everyone stopped giggling to watch her. And when Alistair played the final chord and Rosy finished her last spin, placing her feet into a perfect fifth position, everyone began to clap and cheer.

Having been so nervous about ballet lessons, Rosy was now in her element. It felt brilliant to be the best at something for the first time in her life, and all the other students seemed to be very accepting.

At first they were a bit worried that this new girl would come and get all the attention; Madame Odette did have a bit of a tendency to favouritise new pupils, although thankfully, this time, the slightly batty French woman had, to an extent, left Rosy to get on with it.

This was because she had noticed something in Rosy as soon as the quiet young girl had stepped through the door. Rosy had a kind of aura, a radiating determination to succeed, but also a determination to fit in and to make friends. She had also shown noticeable commitment even before her first lesson, having asked Audrey to teach her some of the steps in order to save time for Madame Odette on the day.

This good idea had also earned Rosy a favourable first impression from the other girls as they got enough attention from the teacher to keep them happy, so really it was smiles all round.

Madame Odette was happy because she had gained a new potential star pupil and Audrey was happy because she had a new best friend. But Rosy perhaps was the happiest of all. Her one wish to have dancing lessons had been granted at last, and she felt that nothing could ever be any more perfect.

***

At the end of the lesson everyone curtsied their thanks to Alistair and to Madame Odette, and then rushed back into the dressing rooms to change back into their everyday clothes.

As Rosy untied her ribbons next to Audrey she felt as if her life suddenly had some meaning. She had made new friends, had a lovely house to live in with her uncle, and now she had proper ballet lessons for two hours every Saturday morning.

She was still in a happy daze when she noticed that Audrey was waving a hand in front of her face, trying to get her attention. "Hello?" she sang, smirking, "anyone at home?" Rosy realised suddenly that they were alone in the dressing room, and she was still only half dressed. "If you hurry up, Rosy, we can walk home together."

A few minutes later the two girls ran down the path and through the gate towards where Audrey's older sister, Evelyn, was leaning up against the crumbling brick wall. She was watching a pair of Buzzards circling against the sky, which, in the course of the ballet lesson, had brightened from a dingy grey to a clear blue hue.

They joined her in watching the birds soaring before Evelyn turned, smiled and spoke. "Hello, I'm Eve, you must be Rosy. Audrey has told me all about you!"

Eve was an extraordinarily beautiful young woman of about twenty with a pretty Highland accent and a radiant smile that showed off her perfectly straight white teeth. Her long blonde hair had been twisted around the sides of her head and gathered at the nape of her neck in an elegant knot, and, following the wartime fashion, she had painted her lips a glamorous red. She was wearing a stylish polka dot dress in exactly the same leafy green colour as her large eyes, which sparkled when she smiled.

"How did you find Madame Odette?" she laughed. "She is a bit of an eccentric, but she has a heart of gold."

"And a very loud laugh!" put in Rosy. Eve explained that she used to attend ballet lessons at the church hall when she was a little girl, until her horse riding, a shining talent of hers, took over.

Rosy could see why Audrey was so proud of Eve. She was very easy to get on with, and more like a friend to her 'little' sister. The Price girls shared the same optimistic approach to life, as well as the same fair hair and green eyes (although Eve's eyes were brighter and her hair a more golden shade of blonde, much to the annoyance of Audrey).

They chatted together all the way back to the road that lead to the campsite, where Audrey gave Rosy a warm hug and then followed her bigger sister down the road towards their farm. When Rosy reached Ivy House she was absolutely shattered, even though it was just time for lunch. Tom was having his lunch up at the campsite because he had some work to finish, but Mrs. McGregor announced that she was "all ears".

Rosy stretched her aching limbs as she excitedly told the housekeeper everything about her morning: about falling over, being the best at pirouettes, and the twins Edine and Faye with their different coloured hair ribbons.

Rosy gabbled rather fast and poor old Mrs. McGregor couldn't really take everything in, but she nodded in all of the right places and rolled her eyes when Rosy came to explaining the 'stunning beauty' of Audrey's sister.

"You'll be like that one day my dear," she

smiled, kindly, shuffling off to fetch some of her famous jam sandwiches that she had prepared for lunch. "Oh I do hope so!" sighed Rosy, dreaming about what her future might hold.

Chapter Seven
IN THE SADDLE

"Come on Rosy it'll be fun!" whined Audrey, pulling one of Rosy's plaits playfully and running away down the hill, dodging the numerous thistle plants and scattered rocks that lay in the long grass. The two girls had been having a picnic on top of the large hill which rose up behind the campsite, and Audrey had just put forward a suggestion about which Rosy was undecided.

"Are you sure that Nessie won't buck or do anything nasty?" Rosy murmered, rolling up the jolly tartan blanket which Mrs. McGregor had lent them for the day, and following her friend, deep in thought. Audrey had suggested that she and Evelyn could take Rosy out for a short ride after their first day back at school the next week, as Evelyn was a qualified instructor and would be happy to give a few lessons for free to her little sister's best friend.

Rosy's creased brow turned slowly into a wide grin as she imagined herself cantering across the landscape, jumping over tangled hedges and splashing through cool, refreshing rivers on the back of the beautiful grey pony, with whom she had become rather affectionate after going to say hello almost every day when visiting Audrey at the farm.

"Alright then," she laughed, then added jokily, "but if I injure myself then it's your fault!"

***

Soon came the time for Rosy's first day at her new school. School in this small Scottish village started each new acedemic year in October, not September, as many of the pupils' fathers were farmers and needed all the help they could get in the fields during the summer harvest. This was one of the first new concepts of many Rosy had to deal with in her new life in the country.

When she walked arm in arm with Audrey through the classroom door, she tried to get her head round the fact that there were only two classes. The first was a class of six children aged from four to ten, and the second, a larger class of about twelve for eleven to sixteen year olds. Having come from her London school with thirty in a class, this new system took a bit of getting used to.

She settled in well because most of her class consisted of the girls from Madame Odette's Ballet School. She recognised the red-headed Morrison twins and took a seat next to them as the ones next to Audrey were already taken. Throughout the day she got on well with the twins. Faye was excellent at mathematics, Rosy's weakest subject, and offered to help her whenever she needed. And Edine proved to be such fun to work with in the English lesson, where they were studying the novel Jane Eyre. She would lark about and put on all the voices and had everyone around her in fits of giggles until the ever-patient teacher told them to get on with their essays. Such hard work was new to Rosy but she found that she soon began to thrive and really quite enjoyed it.

Rosy's class teacher was a kind and enthusiastic woman by the name of Miss Douglas, who was very pleased with her new pupil. She found Rosy cheery and helpful and a pleasure to talk to. Rosy's dancing lifestyle had taught her self-discipline and concentration, skills which were very useful in a classroom environment and which caused her to be much-admired by her fellow pupils even after just one day.

At the lunch break, Audrey took Rosy out to the playing ground behind the school building. Right in the centre there was a massive mossy rock, about the size of a small bungalow, covered in delicate little flowers called sea-pinks. A tree had also taken root on the rock, its knarled trunk twisting up and around it to reach the sunlight. It was an extraordinary sight.

The children were allowed to clamber all over it and it kept them occupied for hours. From a distance they looked somewhat like a pack of monkeys, swarming up the sides and jumping off from a precarious ledge at the top. Rosy was horrified. They would never have been allowed such dangerous things in London. Audrey was grinning proudly, and, gesturing to the boulder with a flourish, she announced, "Our pet rock!"

"A rock?" snorted Rosy. She could tell that the next few years were going to be pretty unusual.

After school the two girls raced as fast as they could down to Allaway Farm where Evelyn was sitting on the fence waiting for them, slowly swinging her jodhpur clad legs and gazing whistfully into the distance.

Underneath all of the dazzling smiles and childlike jokes Evelyn was still a twenty one year old woman, and, despite her closeness to her younger sister, a rather lonely one at times.

Snapping out of her daydream, she jumped nimbly from the fence and ran towards them, pulling them both into a suffocating hug. "Oh girls, I have been waiting all day to take you riding, you can never imagine how dull life can get when all you have to do is mess around with the animals." Rosy thought for a minute and then exclaimed,

"Well, when I am bored I practise some ballet, or sew or something. My uncle's housekeeper has been teaching me needlework." She grinned and then added, proudly, "I've almost finished my first petticoat!"

Evelyn took her little sister's hand and then

quietly began to guide Rosy towards the farm house. "We never learned to sew," she said, almost inaudibly.

"Why?-" started Rosy, intrigued; every girl was taught to sew from an early age, surely.

"Our mother died when Audrey was four," she finished, the twinkle in her eyes fading for one tiny moment.

"Oh, I am so sorry, I didn't realise," murmered Rosy, mortified that she should have brought up a sensitive subject on such a happy, exciting occasion. She felt really quite upset about the whole thing, when suddenly, a quite different feeling flooded coldly over her.

How come Audrey hadn't told her before? Rosy had only known her for just over a month, but already they had become the closest of friends, almost like sisters. They had divulged their deepest secrets and Rosy thought they knew each other inside out.

For one small moment she felt like shouting, "Why didn't you tell me? We're supposed to be best friends." Rosy felt like she suddenly didn't know Audrey. What else was she hiding? Surely, if she had been told earlier, this embarassing situation could have been avoided. She was sure that the lovely Evelyn hated her now for saying such an untactful thing.

Before her imagination had time to take over

completely. Audrey, as if she had heard her friend's thoughts, gently put her hand into Rosy's. "I'm sorry I didn't tell you Rosy, what must you think of me?" she said, pausing as Evelyn fumbled with the stiff latch on the shabbily painted farm house door. "You understand, don't you? It's still very hard to talk about, but it's about time I opened up to you, isn't it?"

Rosy gripped Audrey's hand and smiled gratefully, now feeling somehow more awful for being so naive. Yet another strong emotion now hit Rosy. She felt guilty that she could ever feel so selfish towards Audrey, one of the most generous, accepting people she had ever met. Audrey had welcomed Rosy whole-heartedly into her life, as had everybody else in the tight-knit community.

"Please don't worry about it," put in Evelyn, reassuringly, the twinkle restored to her eyes, "We are here to have a lot of fun, and that is exactly what I intend to do!"

***

Ten minutes later Rosy emerged from the farmhouse, now fully kitted out in a pair of Audrey's jodhpurs with her school blouse tucked neatly into the belt. She also had on a pair of Audrey's old knee-length riding boots. Luckily, her shoe size was just a bit smaller than her friend's, although the two were practically the same height.

Wasting no time, the similarly attired Audrey grabbed Rosy's hand and dragged her down to the stables where Evelyn had already gone to prepare the horses, although not before making Rosy feel suitably embarrassed by commenting on how smart she looked in a riding hat.

As they made their way to the tumbledown stable block, Rosy was getting ever more nervous about the prospect of riding a horse for the first time in her life. Although she had now become quite comfortable around the gentle animals, Evelyn had a rather difficult task to increase Rosy's confidence enough for her to sit on the horse and walk around.

Soon the horses were ready to be mounted, and Evelyn took Rosy gently by the hand leading her over to Nessie, who's gorgeous glossy grey hair had been brushed vigorously for the occassion until it shone like silver in the light of the sun, which was growing increasingly brighter as the afternoon drew on.

Noticing Rosy's tense, nervous expression, Evelyn smiled kindly. "Truly, you'll be fine, I know you have the determination to do this. I've heard about your persistence in ballet. You went from not knowing a single step to being the best dancer in the class." At this point Rosy blushed a light pink but kept silent; now was not the right time for an outburst of modesty.

Evelyn carried on in the same soft tone, and succeeded in slightly reassuring the now shaking twelve year old.

"If you could make those initial brave steps in dance, your first pirouette for instance, that must have been daunting?" Rosy nodded obediently. "Well, a pirouette takes great posture, alignment and coordination, but after you've tried it once, these things seem easier." Rosy was impressed by Evelyn's technical vocabulary, as was Evelyn's sister, who grinned enthusiastically.

"You should have been a ballet teacher!" she laughed.

"But seriously, horse riding can't be much different to learning ballet."

"Yes, but ballet doesn't involve being on top of a large moving creature with a mind of its own!" Rosy protested, starting to have second thoughts about the whole idea. She had, after all, never actually been so close to a horse until a month ago. It was only natural for her to be feeling extremely anxious.

After a few minutes of calm coaxing, Rosy had finally allowed herself to be helped onto the back of the placid grey pony, and as soon as she felt the familiar sofness of Nessie's mane all her previous fears vanished and she began to get used to the strange feeling of the horse's body moving underneath her.

With Evelyn guiding her along on a short leading rope, and Audrey just behind her on her own chestnut pony, Rosy was introduced to this exhilarating activity in so much more of a fun and relaxed way than if she had taken lessons anywhere else. "It is so handy that my friends can teach me," she thought to herself, "this is just perfect."

Soon she began to really enjoy it, letting her body really go with the motions of the horse's swaying movements. "Wow Rosy! You're a natural!" praised Evelyn, stopping to pick a blackberry from the surrounding bushes. Nessie stretched her head forward to receive it, putting Rosy off balance.

She tipped forwards with a cry of surprise, and ended up hugging the horse's neck rather ungracefully. When Evelyn turned back round and saw her in this uncomfortable position she tossed her long golden plait behind her and laughed at Rosy's shocked expression.

"Oh, dear, that does look awkward, all you have to do is pull her head back with the reins." Rosy was indignant.

"You could have told me before I made a fool out of myself!" she pouted.

"Never mind, you'll get to learn these things," grinned Evelyn, "But now seems like a good time to dismount and have a spot of lunch!"

Chapter Eight
THE EXCITEMENT NEVER STOPS

After helping Rosy to swing herself from the saddle, Evelyn removed the rucksack from her back, threw it at her sister to unpack and went to find a suitable place to tie the horses up. "Eve has been really lonely recently," whispered Audrey, "She does enjoy doing things with us, but I think she needs someone more her age to be around some of the time."

Rosy nodded, although she didn't really understand. How can such a lively, cheerful woman be so unhappy inside? "There isn't anybody her age in the village anymore," continued Audrey, "all the young men have gone off to fight in the war."

"Uncle Tom hasn't," interrupted Rosy, "He has a weak heart so the doctors wouldn't let him go."

"Yes but he's old," exclaimed Audrey, grinning wickedly at Rosy's now somewhat defensive air. "He's thirty five!" At this point, Evelyn returned, having tied the horses to sturdy branches of an old apple tree, and the three of them sat down beneath it to eat the splendid picnic she had prepared for them while they were at school.

Sitting on the soil in the shade beneath the leafy

tree, Rosy could see right out over the rising and falling fields, meadows, hills and valleys, and in the distance she could just see the sea, a hazy sapphire ribbon stretching out across the horizon. The landscape was like a patchwork quilt in dozens of different hues of brown and green, dotted here and there with cotton-wool sheep.

The scene was bathed in shimmering sunshine and the sky was a delicate blue, adorned with fluffy white clouds. Where there were trees long shadows stretched across the rocky ground. Under their tree the sunlight filtered through the gently swaying leaves, making golden patterns dance on their skin. Rosy shut her eyes and let the warmth spread from her face to the rest of her body.

Her meditation was interrupted by an exclamation from Audrey. "Are you going to eat any food or aren't you?" She then poked Rosy, and smirked, chucking an apple at her.

"Ouch, that hurt! Yes, sorry, this is a gorgeous picnic," Rosy giggled, "I was just thinking how warm it is for October. I thought Scotland was supposed to be wet and rainy!" Evelyn frowned.

"Sometimes it does seem to rain every day, but we've had a bit of a drought this year. That downpour on the first day you arrived here was the first rain we had seen in six weeks. Father was tearing his hair out because his crops would have died if it hadn't rained, and soon."

She shook her head, and her hardened features relaxed. "Tuck in!"

It was amazing how much food could be stuffed into a small backpack. There were jam sandwiches, apples, large pieces of cheese, blackberry pies and two small chocolate bars to share between them. Chocolate was an indulgence, even for Audrey and Evelyn, as it was so expensive.

Living out in the middle of nowhere meant that you had to rely on the crops that the local farmers grew. For treats like chocolate and sweets, there was always a hope that the village store had ordered some in from the nearest town, Inverness, which was a four hour drive away.

"Make the most of this, won't you," reminded Evelyn. "We will have to be careful what and how much we eat. Some things are becoming very hard to get hold of and will have to be reserved for special occasions."

"But this is a special occasion," cried Audrey, "This is Rosy's first riding lesson!" Evelyn smiled, and hugged Rosy.

"That's true."

***

About half an hour later, all the picnic things had been packed away and Rosy had been helped again onto Nessie's back. "Is it alright if I go ahead and canter? Bobby's getting a bit fidgety," asked Audrey, pulling back impatiently on the reins of her chestnut pony, who was pawing the ground and emitting loud snorts from his rippling nostrils.

Rosy found this horse's behaviour rather frightening and readily agreed, watching her friend canter quickly down the dusty track with great awe and fascination. She found just walking difficult and daunting.

Noticing Rosy's admiring face, Evelyn laughed in her friendly way, "You'll get there one day!" before making a gentle clicking sound with her mouth and urging Nessie on. The further Rosy rode, the more she began to relax and enjoy it.

She loved the feeling of being able to see over the tops of the tangled bramble hedges, and was mastering the knack of pulling back on the reins lightly to stop the pony from reaching out its elegant silver neck over to the brambles to eat any ripe blackberries that had not yet been picked by the village children.

Now, the rocking motion of the pony's gait seemed almost completely natural to Rosy, having found it stiff and uncomfortable only a few hours before. Evelyn and Rosy travelled along the winding pathways happily without a word.

The only sound to be heard was the dull rhythmic thud of Nessie's hooves on the soil track and the occasional outbreak of birdsong from the trees above. Suddenly, Evelyn stopped in her tracks, and pointed over to the field which they were passing.

"Look Rosy, over there, by that fence!" Standing tall and majestic only a few yards away from them was a magnificent red deer stag with spiked antlers the length of a person's arms, huge questioning eyes, and long, powerful legs.

His velvet coat was a rich reddish brown colour and an autumn mane of thick, dark hair was beginning to grow around his neck. Rosy recognised it from one of her uncle's paintings in Ivy House, but never thought she would be lucky enough to see one in the flesh so soon after moving to Scotland.

Rosy dared not breathe as the stag stared loftily at them for several seconds before abruptly turning and bolting away. This sudden movement caused a frightened Nessie to rear up on her hind legs uncontrollably, tossing her head and whinnying with wild eyes.

Rosy yelled and fell backwards hitting the ground with a thump and a cloud of dust.

"Rosy! Are you hurt?" cried a panicked Evelyn, calming the pony then rushing over to tend to Rosy, who sat up slowly, nodding her head.

"I'm fine, really," she said, "just a bit shaken." Evelyn helped her to her feet and Rosy brushed the dirt off her jodhpurs, comfortingly stroking Nessie's muzzle. "It's alright now Nessie, the scary deer's gone."

Evelyn looked on, impressed at the young girl's calmness, and her sense to make sure that the horse was all right first before tending to her own needs. "Rosy, you are a dear!" she smiled, more relieved if anything that Rosy had not been seriously hurt while in her care.

The only minor pain that Rosy could feel was a slight throbbing in the forefinger of her left hand. She assumed that she must have twisted it when she fell to the ground. It didn't bother her at all as being a dancer meant that she always had some form of cramp, strain or other completely unexplained pain somewhere in her body.

Furthermore, her first proper riding fall had somehow changed her attitude. Rosy had realised that a horse could be just as scared as she was. Nessie had proved that to her when she had spooked at the sudden movement of the deer.

Suddenly she felt a sincere understanding towards the pony that now stood next to her, affectionately rubbing her head against the sleeve of Rosy's blouse.

And it was this understanding that allowed Rosy to return bravely to the saddle (after a worried Evelyn had made absolutely sure that both girl and pony were perfectly fine) and ride with confidence back to Allaway farm where she reluctantly swapped back Audrey's jodhpurs for her own woollen school kilt.

***

Rosy whimpered pathetically, letting Mrs. McGregor place her finger against a paper-clad ice cube, wincing as the cold shot through her finger like a thousand tiny needles penetrating her skin.

Her uncle was pacing up and down behind the chair that she was sitting on, an annoyed expression looking somewhat out of place on his handsome face.

"Who exactly was it that went out with you?" he asked, frowning. Rosy replied nervously,

"Audrey and her big sister Evelyn, I did tell you when I asked you if I could go."

"Oh, what, Evelyn the 'stunning beauty'?" smiled Mrs. McGregor with an amused gleam in her sea blue eyes which faded as Tom carried on with his pacing.

"I don't see what that has to do with anything Effie, the point is it's..." he scowled as he searched for the correct word.

"Irresponsible, that's what it is, irresponsible!" he spluttered, still walking with long heavy strides back and forth.

"Would you be so kind as to stop with the pacing Tom, I'm feeling a wee bit dizzy," interrupted Mrs. McGregor quietly, sorting out Rosy's now considerably more swollen finger before sinking into a chair with a soft groan and the creaking of ancient joints.

"Evelyn, or whatever her name is, should know better," continued Tom, getting more and more annoyed with each word, "I mean, poor Rosy has never ridden a horse before."

"I'm not poor, I'm perfectly fine."

Mrs. McGregor sighed deeply, "Tom, young Evelyn is a qualified horse riding instructor, and you know it. She could not have done anything to stop the horse from spooking now could she?" Rosy looked from the determined old woman to her uncle, resorting to begging upon seeing his still stony expression.

"Eve said that the best thing to stop me from being put off is to get straight back on or I'd never have gone on a horse again and that woud be really sad because I started to enjoy myself so much. I said my finger was alright because it really was then. It wasn't Eve's fault Tom, please don't be angry with her!"

Tom folded his arms defensively. "I'm not angry. You could have been seriously hurt. I'm just mildly annoyed." Mrs. McGregor shared a cynical look with Rosy then smirked,

"Really? We'd never have noticed." Tom glared at her for a while before making up his mind,

"I shall speak to Evelyn when I pick you up from that birthday party tomorrow, Mr. Price will be working on the farm I believe, so I assume *she* will be picking Audrey up."

Forgetting about her friend Evelyn's inpending fate, Rosy's face lit up as she suddenly remembered the party to which she had been invited. It was to take place at the Morrison twins' house by the beach for their twelfth birthday celebration.

"Oh goody! The party, I had forgotten about that!" she shrieked, the pain of her swollen finger seeming to disappear rapidly. "Come, Effie, you must help me pick something to wear!" The housekeeper creaked back to her feet with another sigh.

"I'm getting too old for this," she murmered, "does the excitement never stop?"

Chapter Nine
A FAILED COMPLAINT

Singing happily, and greedily gulping in the fresh scent of the sea air, Rosy skipped down the hill from the campsite. A tired Mrs. McGregor huffed and puffed behind her, trying to keep up with the sprightly little girl's bounds.

Rosy posé-turned down the path, laughing happily as the skirt of her dress flared out in almost a full circle around her.

She was dressed in her smartest party attire, a pretty lilac dress underneath her prized red coat, and her shiny white leather shoes. She had discarded her everyday white ankle socks and donned her first pair of stockings for the occasion. They looked quite elegant on her now well-toned dancer's legs.

To complete the look she had slid her crimson satin rose into her hair, which hung loose around her shoulders, and, of course, her silver locket hung proudly around her neck.

Rosy had been invited the Morrison twins' party, and was very excited. The parties she had been to at home in London only involved a few games and a tea, before the guests were ushered home. This party was going to be so much better!

As the twins had a huge garden at the back of their equally huge house, all the guests were going to stay overnight in a tent on the lawn. Games of cricket and pass-the-parcel were promised and for dinner they were going to bake potatoes on a campfire.

Rosy could hardly contain her excitement! She sprinted the last few yards to the house, and waited for Mrs. McGregor to catch up before eagerly ringing the door bell.

She was surprised to find the door open a matter of seconds later, and nine pairs of hands grabbed her, hauling her inside. The other girls must have been waiting by the door for her to arrive. She shouted her goodbyes to Mrs. McGregor and let herself be dragged over the threshold and hugged enthusiastically. "Rosy, finally you're here. We haven't seen you forever!"

"What, since yesterday?" she giggled, hurriedly taking off her coat, hanging it next to the others and handing neatly wrapped presents of home-made jams to the twins. All the other guests were in her class at school, and they were also all in Madame Odette's dance class.

Audrey was there, alongside Clara, Logan, Fiona, Frankie, Jane, and of course Edine and Faye themselves. They were both red- faced with excitement and showing off two beautiful antique silk scarves, green and violet respectively, which they had been given by their grandmother.

By five o'clock the girls had finished their fervent game of cricket and the sunlight was starting to fade, so Mr. Morrison decided that it was time to get the campfire built on the beach before it was too dark to see what they were doing.

The group were asked to go off and find bits of wood on the ground beneath the trees that stood, tall and shadowy, next to the road opposite the beach. They ran off, the sound of their singing and laughter ringing out across the bay, bringing joy to the ears of all who heard the sound.

Half an hour later they returned to the beach with arms full of twigs and branches, to find Mr. Morrison digging a shallow hole in the sand and bordering it with stones. The girls' sticks were placed in a large mound with his help, and then he lit a few matches, dropping them one by one onto the pile. The flames started to lick the dry bark, creeping steadily higher, until, as the daylight gradually faded, the fire became gradually bigger and brighter.

In a few minutes the smouldering pile of twigs had grown to a boisterous blaze, the flames dancing and leaping as the girls themselves leaped and danced around it in a bizarre tribal fashion. Their cavorting was interrupted by a shout from Mr. Morrison to his daughters.

"Message from your mother – would the

strange fire sprites like their dinner?" This was met with ten grateful nods and exclamations of, "Oh, yes please!" The partiers had built up quite an appetite in the last three hours and were greatly looking forward to their feast.

Ten minutes later, the group were sitting quietly round the campfire, tucking into piping hot potatoes and watching the crackling sparks fly swiftly into the night sky. Rosy let out a contented sigh. "This is the best party I have ever been to in my whole life!" she exclaimed, brushing the crumbs off her lap onto the sand and beaming fit to burst.

**

It was about two o'clock in the morning, and a quiet whispering, occasionally broken by a shrill giggle and urgent 'shh's, could be heard coming from the large canvas tent in the Morrison's garden. The giggling continued, this time stopped by the eerie hoot of an owl which floated through the autumn air across the countryside, startling the girls for a second.

Inside the tent it was completely dark, although during the night the girls' eyes had become accustomed to this lack of light, and they could just about make out the vague outlines of each other's faces in order to have a conversation.

They had been instructed to try to keep quiet,

which they were finding quite hard to do, and also to try to get some sleep, which definitely wasn't happening!

This was everyone's first sleepover together, and they all harboured some curious determination to stay awake all through the night, a skill that was coming easily to them. As the hours drew on, they never ran out of things to talk about, or seemed to get any more tired, and soon they heard the first bird song of the morning, a lonely thrush twittering clear and strong.

"Shh! Listen!" Whispered Edine, excitedly, "A bird!"

"Ahh!" sighed Rosy. "Beautiful." They sat in silence for a minute and listened to the sounds of the morning. The tide had come in, the relaxing sound of the waves crashing on the shore getting steadily louder, and more birds joining the first in song.

"I know!" exclaimed Faye, jumping to her feet. "Do let's go and watch the sun rise from the sea shore, it'll be gorgeous." After several groans from the warm and comfortable girls, they all managed to stretch and step out into the crisp morning, dragging their bulky blankets behind them.

They sat tucked in their blankets in a row on the turf at the shore-line (which stretched along the bottom of the garden) and they watched in silence as the great orange sun slowly appeared over the hills behind them, bathing the sea in a delicate pinkish glow. Two sailing boats passed by and disappeared into the distance, followed by a noisy, silhouetted gaggle of geese.

It was the most beautiful sight that Rosy had ever seen. "I wish mother and father could see this," she thought to herself, then spoke out loud: "I am so lucky to be living here, this is beyond amazing!"

Audrey murmured in response, "It is such a strange feeling. It sounds clichéd, I know, but it's like I've woken up to a beautiful new life."

"Not that we've actually woken up, we were already awake!" corrected Jane, laughing.

"I reckon I am going to appreciate where I live so much more now." Audrey smiled, putting an arm around Rosy. "We *are* lucky to be living here, and this is the most wonderful time of day to appreciate it, I feel like we're the only people awake in the village."

"We probably are," put in Faye, checking her new birthday wristwatch. "It's half past five in the morning!"

***

By eleven o'clock, four parents and siblings had arrived and collected their exhausted girls. The remaining guests and the twins were now lying flat out on the grass in the front garden of the magnificent house, too tired to chat, just enjoying each others' company.

They all looked up as they heard another pair of feet crunching on the gravel, and Rosy grimaced as she noticed Tom striding purposefully towards the house.

"Hello girls!" he smiled, although his mind was clearly on other things. He sat down on the garden bench with a sigh. He wanted to talk to Evelyn about letting Rosy back on to the horse the day before after hurting herself, and he knew *exactly* what he was going to say.

Just then Evelyn came into view and walked elegantly up the path towards them, noticing Tom, who leapt to his feet in an instant."Hello, you must be Tom!" she said, tucking a lock of her golden hair behind her ear with a dazzling smile.

"Err...hello!" he stuttered, unable to take his eyes off her. Suddenly, his mind went blank and he had no idea what he was supposed to be saying. He ran his hand through his messy mop of hair making it stick up endearingly, and stammered again.

Rosy held her breath. Why wasn't he having a go at her like he said he would? She glanced over at Audrey who knelt up, grinned, and widened her eyes in disbelief. Rosy looked back at Evelyn, who was standing there fondly smiling at Tom.

"We'll just make a start home, shall we?" grinned Rosy, thanking the twins' parents, hugging the other girls and grabbing Audrey.

They made their way down the road, trying to conceal their giggles as the adults talked a few steps behind. When they reached the turning for the campsite Tom smiled and turned to Evelyn. "Will you be picking Audrey up from ballet tomorrow?" he asked, hopefully.

"Yes," she replied, "I will." They stood and smiled at each other again before turning and going their separate ways.

As they walked down the lane, Audrey nudged her sister. "Rosy's uncle Tom is handsome, isn't he?"

"Is he?" came the reply, the young woman's effort to conceal her emotions failing completely as she blushed crimson, much to Audrey's amusement.

When Rosy and Tom reached Ivy House Mrs. McGregor was in the front garden, weeding. "Did you talk to Evelyn?" she questioned, confused at his rapturous expression.

"What about?" he replied. The old woman raised her eyebrows.

"So, the woman being stunningly beautiful has "nothing to do with anything" does it?"

Chapter Ten
THE FIRST STEP TO STARDOM

"What do you think, Rosy?" implored Audrey, walking backwards in front of her friend, determined to extract Rosy's true opinion on a serious matter concerning the upcoming ballet school show.

"I've told you, I don't know," Rosy whined, rubbing her hands together to warm them and stuffing them in her pockets. "I haven't been at the school for long." Audrey cried out in anguish,

"But you'll get the part with no trouble."

"That's my point Audrey. Here I come swanning into their ballet school, a complete newcomer. If I got the part I'd feel awful."

The two friends were walking home from their dancing class, at which Madame Odette had given them the exciting news that they were to put on a show on Christmas Eve, which was now only two months away.

The show was to be 'Robin Hood', and you could say that it was a sort of a ballet pantomime as the lead part of Robin was to be played by a girl, and a boy would take the part of the Lady Marion's outrageous lady in waiting. Rosy had been encouraged to go for Robin, but being a rather modest and thoughtful person she was having serious doubts.

"That's your problem my friend," sighed Audrey, stopping in the middle of the road and grabbing Rosy's arm. "You need to realise that you have talent. Grab the opportunity. No one else cares so much about ballet as you do. *We* only do it for fun."

"So do I," exclaimed Rosy, shaking her arm free and continuing to walk, her brow screwed up in concentration. She began to dribble a small, round pebble along the road, each kick sending up a cloud of dust that hung in the dense air like the mist that often rolled down from the surrounding mountains on cold autumn mornings.

"Well, I don't know. What other twelve year old girl would spend every second of their spare time practising ballet and not want to do it professionally?" Audrey stopped again, frowning. "Don't tell me you hadn't thought about being a ballet dancer." Rosy blinked, deep in thought,

"I guess the notion had crossed my mind," she murmured. "I've been too busy concentrating on the present to worry about the future. But come to think of it, I can't see myself doing anything else!"

She linked arms with Audrey, continuing to kick her stone until she kicked too hard and it rolled into the overgrown, brambly ditch and out of sight.

"Do you think I'd be good enough?" Audrey smiled warmly,

"Rosy, it would be a crime for you not to be a ballet dancer."

When they reached campsite turning, red-nosed and cold-footed, a triumphant Audrey had finally persuaded Rosy to try for the part, and Rosy was secretly quite looking forward to it.

It would be her first time on the stage, and the thought of it enthralled her; the lights, makeup and a captivated audience appealed to the outgoing, extrovert part of her personality.

By the time she had reached Ivy House and sunk into a squishy armchair by the fire in the living room, the familiar feeling of overwhelming determination had returned to her, and nothing could stop her from getting the part.

***

"Thank you children, you can go home for lunch and then I will 'ave you back 'ere at two o'clock when I shall give you the results of the auditions!" Madame Odette finished her speech and hurried her pupils out of the hall where she began to consult with the pianist, Alistair, and a slim mousy lady, Irene, who assisted the teacher with the younger students.

The twenty or so children who had auditioned

dispersed nervously back to their homes. Rosy and Audrey joined Evelyn at Allaway farm for soup and bread, most of which lay still untouched half an hour later.

Poor Evelyn tried her best to make conversation and lighten the mood, but to no avail. At half past one, the girls got up to start on the walk back to the church hall, after having eaten almost nothing due to nerves.

"Off you go then girls," smiled Evelyn, ushering them out of the door and into the dull landscape. "Good luck, both of you! I'll be down to pick you up Audrey in an hour," she called after the silent pair as they trudged down the lane, her silvery voice echoing comfortingly across the bay.

Rosy felt perhaps the more anxious of the two. She had gone for a principal character, and the shyer Audrey a corps de ballet part. Although it was only a small-scale Christmas show in a tiny village tucked away in the highlands of Scotland, it felt to Rosy like the first step of her career. Since Audrey had mentioned being a professional ballet dancer, Rosy had been able to think of nothing else.

It felt to her as though she had never wanted anything else in her life, and she was now working harder in her ballet classes than ever. She had a sudden yearning to perform, to show people what she could do, and if she got the title role in this show it would be the first step to stardom!

A brisk walk and a nervous wait later, the children were all called back into the hall for the cast to be announced. Audrey and Rosy held each other's hands as Madame Odette began to speak.

"Now I'm pleased to announce that everybody who auditioned for our show will be taking part." Rosy relaxed. She would definitely be on the stage at Christmas, no matter how small her role. Madame Odette carried on, her soft French accent going some way to calm the air of impatience and tension that was lying like a stifling cloak over the pupils. "It will be a relatively big cast so lots of concentration will be required from all of you."

"Now, I will read out the names of the girls in the corps," she continued. The tension lifted child by child as their names were called out. As the gracious teacher finished her list of the fifteen girls in the corps de ballet, Rosy's excitement swelled. She realised that, as she had not been cast in the corps, she must have at least a solo part.

Audrey dropped her hand from Rosy's; her name had not been called either. She turned, distressed, to Rosy, who reassured her friend, beaming widely.

"Madame Odette said that everyone had a part," she grinned. "That can only mean..."

"The part of the Lady Marion will be played by Audrey Price," came the pronouncement, at which point Audrey's jaw dropped almost to the floor.

"But I only auditioned for the corps!" she whispered, astounded.

"Why are you so worried?" giggled Rosy, "you got a principal part!" She sighed at Audrey's shocked expression, not even daring to hope as her name continued not to be called out.

"And finally, the role of Robin will be given to Rosy Lane! Well done everybody. From now on normal classes will be discontinued and rehearsals will take place twice a week in this hall." Rosy's heart stopped.

She had done it! Her first proper show and the main part too. She could hardly contain her excitement. She wanted more than anything to grab Audrey's hands and jump up and down, but she could tell that something was troubling her best friend.

As the loudly chattering cast filed out of the hall, Audrey shyly approached Madame Odette. "Madame, I only auditioned for a corps part, I don't think I can handle Lady Marion." The kindly French woman put her hands on the wide-eyed girl's shoulders.

"It will be a challenge for you, Miss Price, 'owever I would not 'ave put you in the part if I did not think you were capable." Audrey smiled gratefully, before running over to join Rosy by the doors. Now pure excitement replaced her previous concern.

They skipped ecstatically out of the building to the front gate, where they found Tom and Evelyn deep in conversation. They both looked up as they heard the giggles and squeals of delight from the two girls, who joined hands and span round the adults singing, "We're to play Robin Hood and Maid Marion, oh what fun it shall be!" Evelyn put her hand out to stop her little sister, who had become quite pink with excitement.

"I thought you only went for a corps part," she questioned, but before Audrey could answer, Rosy cut in.

"Audrey misjudged herself, Eve, Madame Odette promoted her to principal!" Tom was delighted.

"Well, this is definitely a cause for celebration! Evelyn, would you and Audrey like to come back to the campsite and have some tea with us? My housekeeper has made a great big fruit pie which I'd love to share with somebody."

Evelyn sighed and smiled, appreciatively. "Thank you, but Audrey and I really should be going. Father's gone to stay with his sister in Glasgow for the month, so I'm cooking." A flicker of disappointment appeared very clearly on Tom's face.

"Do you have to go home straight away?" he faltered, running his hand through his hair as he often did when in an awkward situation.

"Oh please, Eve, I haven't had tea at the campsite for such a long time, besides, Rosy and I have lots to talk about," Audrey pleaded.

"We have real cream," added Tom.

"Well in that case!" Evelyn wasn't too hard to win over and soon the four of them were walking briskly up the hill, spurred on by the thought of cream and hot fruit pie on such a chilly autumn day.

When they reached Ivy House, Rosy and Audrey rushed straight up to the attic bedroom to talk about the ballet show. After making a pot of tea, Tom and Evelyn found Mrs. McGregor at Tom's desk, her horn-rimmed glasses perched on the end of her long beaklike nose and her tiny frame swamped by paperwork.

"Tom, we need to talk about the campsite's finances, we really are in great trouble..." She span rapidly around to face them, the ancient leather office chair creaking in complaint. "Oh! Sorry, I didn't realise you had company," she exclaimed, looking the slender figure of Evelyn up and down, taking in the luscious blonde curls and sparkling green eyes.

"This must be Evelyn," she said, standing up to shake the intrigued woman's hand. Evelyn was fascinated by the living room.

"Well, this is amazing, I wish our living room was this cosy. Since my mother died our house has become dark and stuffy, and I don't think I'll ever get round to doing anything about it. Anyway, are you sure we're not intruding?"

Tom sank into the sofa, gesturing to the seat next to him, which Evelyn took, gratefully. "Intruding?" he frowned, "Oh yes, the finances. No, if you don't mind, Effie can talk it over now."

Evelyn nodded, sipping her steaming mug of revitalising tea and trying not to listen in too much on the important conversation that was now taking place between the old housekeeper and Tom.

Mrs. McGregor explained that since the war had started fewer people were going on holiday, so the campsite was suffering a severe lack of customers. And now rationing had been brought in, Ivy House was becoming harder and harder to support.

"We need more money coming in, and fast," she finished, before bustling off to call the girls down for their tea.

Tom's hair was now sticking up like a chimney brush and his tie hung undone around his neck; he had hit a serious stumbling-block and could not see a way out of this grave situation.

Evelyn sat slightly awkwardly with her tea until Mrs. McGregor called them through to the kitchen, where Rosy and Audrey were already seated, eagerly awaiting their feast.

As they tucked into their deep slices of pie and cream (a real delicacy in a time of heavy rationing)

Evelyn was thinking hard. "Tom, I don't want to interfere, but I've had an idea." Tom sat up, immediately attentive. He was willing to try anything that would save his struggling business.

"This pie is fantastic, Mrs. McGregor," she clarified, "You know, I think you could sell these!"

Rosy joined in enthusiastically, "Yes! We could start up a café down in the village or something."

Mrs. McGregor stood up suddenly. "We can grow most things, like fruit, ourselves, it wouldn't cost us much."

"Ivy Café!" laughed Evelyn. "We'll help you set it up, it'll be fun!" She looked at Tom, who was smiling as if his life had just been given back to him.

"It could work!" he gasped, his eyes shining brightly as he hastily re-knotted his tie and grabbed his coat.

"Where are you going?" demanded Mrs. McGregor, sweeping the plates into the sink.

"To the Post Office," Tom replied, dashing out of the room without another word.

A confused Evelyn, Audrey, Rosy and housekeeper were left sitting silently in the kitchen. "To the Post Office?" they murmured to each other, no one becoming any more enlightened as to why.

"Of course!" Evelyn jumped up. "The old store building," she grinned, before grabbing her coat and running down to the bay after Tom. Rosy and Audrey weren't going to miss out on the fun at any costs.

As they caught up with the adults, who were already in conference with the amiable Post Master, they knew that their next few months would be the busiest of their lives.

Not only would they have demanding rehearsals for the ballet school show, but it now looked as though they would be required to help out on a new and exciting project!

Chapter Eleven
TOM DISCOVERED

Over the next few weeks Tom, Evelyn, Mrs. McGregor, Audrey and Rosy worked so hard that time soon began to creep up on them. Before they knew it, there were only a few days to go until Christmas. The two girls had been rehearsing intensively for their roles in Madame Odette's ballet show, and they now knew their parts back to front and inside out.

In between their twice-weekly rehearsals, Rosy and Audrey had been trying their best to help get the new café open in time for the annual Christmas Eve celebrations. Now the school holidays had come they were able to help whenever they were not down at the church hall or in the disused dining room at Ivy House, which was the perfect space for practising dances.

In the first few days after Evelyn had the idea for the café, Tom had managed to buy the ancient, tumbledown outbuilding from the postmaster for a reasonable price.

He had set straight to work, with the help of Evelyn whenever she could find the time, knocking down, rebuilding and painting, day in, day out.

While he had been doing all this, Mrs. McGregor had kindly offered to look after the running of another new scheme: bed and breakfast at Ivy House, so Rosy had been suffering Tom's cooking since the start of the project.

Rosy had also hatched another plan in order to help her uncle's finances. She had started to give up most of her free time to work for Evelyn down at the Allaway Farm stables in order to make a bit of money.

She could then pay for her own ballet lessons and save Tom the expense. Being down at the stables more also meant that she had the opportunity to ride the horses more often, and was now becoming quite good at it.

She had a wonderful ability to communicate with the horses well, and this made her a natural horsewoman. Evelyn would come home from the café to find Rosy riding round and round the arena on Nessie, practising rising trot and circles until they were perfect.

She had discovered through her ballet training that something could be improved by repetition and this was the approach that she took with her riding. She would only stop when Nessie tired, and only then for the horse's wellbeing; she would have practised all night if she could.

One lunchtime, when Tom was hard at work in the café down at the bay, Mrs. McGregor had a surprise for Rosy. "I was talking to your uncle last night," she said, handing Rosy a plate of steaming shepherd's pie, and sitting down with her own plate next to her.

"Oh yes," nodded Rosy, absently blowing on her meal to cool it, blinking rapidly as the steam spiralled into her eyes; she was not really listening at all.

"It's about your ballet," the old housekeeper continued. Rosy's head sprang up and her eyes widened. Now Mrs. McGregor had her full attention. "It has come to Madame Odette's knowledge that you are taking riding lessons and she advises you to stop." Rosy's jaw dropped.

"What?" she gasped, leaping to her feet, then immediately sinking back down into the chair with a groan. "Why?"

"Horse riding develops the wrong kind of muscles for dancing, and apparently if you want to pursue a career in ballet, it is unadvisable to ride at all." Rosy pushed her plate away, speechless, her appetite completely extinguished.

"What did Tom say?" she demanded, her shepherd's pie sitting forgotten on the table.

"You'll have to ask him," frowned Mrs. McGregor, pushing Rosy's lunch back towards her and encouraging her to take a bite, to no avail. Rosy was determined to find out if she could still ride.

She had grown to love it over the last few

months and did not intend to give it up so soon.

"He did seem quite reluctant to stop you from going I must admit." Mrs. McGregor added, thoughtfully, "though I am not sure your outstanding dedication to your hobbies is much to do with it."

"I'm not with you," said Rosy, gazing questioningly at the housekeeper.

"I think that your uncle rather enjoys the regular meetings with young Audrey's sister that picking you up from the farm entails," smirked Mrs. McGregor.

"But that's absurd!" exclaimed Rosy, choking on a mouthful of mashed potato. "It's Evelyn!" Mrs. McGregor laughed, handing the spluttering Rosy a glass of water.

"Well, it's obvious that you love to dance more than anything, so you and your uncle will have to make a compromise." Rosy nodded, reluctantly. "I'll talk to Madame Odette tonight," she decided, her exhausted brain now presented with more tricky decisions.

"I think I should miss riding if I had to give it up," she contemplated, finally finishing her pie and handing it to Mrs. McGregor for washing up.

"I'm sure it won't come to that," the housekeeper reassured her. "Tom won't let it!"

***

After that evening's rehearsal Rosy nervously approached an understanding Madame Odette, who repeated what she had said to Tom the day before. "All I am saying is that I feel that it would benefit your career if you reduced your horse riding. It is a well known fact that ballet and riding should not be mixed."

"My career?" murmured Rosy, and as her heart stopped in apprehension she realised that she was wanting the teacher to say something to the effect of...

"Rosy, with enough training, I think that you have the potential to become a professional ballet dancer," nodded Madame Odette with evident pride. Rosy felt her cheeks flush with happiness, and she found herself hugging the amused teacher tightly around the waist. She had been waiting for that important reassurance from someone who really knew what they were talking about.

It was one thing being told that you are really good by a friend, but in showing her confidence, Madame Odette had also given the motivated Rosy confidence in her dream. In the course of that conversation, the young girl's ambition seemed that one step closer, that one bit more attainable.

Since speaking with Audrey before the ballet show audition, Rosy's mind had been buzzing with a mixture of excitement and nervousness. She had never really thought so much about her future, however as the days went by, she had become increasingly intent on becoming a ballet dancer, a career that she knew would be almost as difficult and painful as it would be rewarding.

To dedicate your whole life to dancing is a choice not entered into lightly. Rosy knew that, which is why she was so relieved to be told she was good enough by Madame Odette. She was not setting her hopes on something completely unachievable to her. Now there was absolutely nothing to stop her from dancing!

That evening Tom arrived home at ten o'clock, covered in splatters of paint as usual and with bits of dust clinging to his already unkempt mop of hair. Rosy was stretching with her leg up the living room wall when he burst through the door with gleaming eyes and announced that the café was ready to be decorated, the enjoyable task that all of the helpers had been waiting for.

"Oh, hooray!" yelped Rosy, springing to her feet, already brimming with ideas. "Let's paint it green, ivy green!"

"Whoa!" exclaimed Tom, pushing the enthusiastic child towards the staircase. "Right now it's your bed time, we can discuss the café in the morning." When they reached the bottom of the stairs Rosy span round to face her uncle.

"I have reached a compromise!" she announced, waiting expectantly for an answer.

"Oh brilliant!" Tom nodded, before frowning. "What about?" Rosy sighed, pushing her uncle to the bottom step and sitting heavily next to him.

"Oh Tom, don't you remember?" she whined. "About my riding."

"Oh, yes, I'd forgotten about that." Which was true; her uncle had spent every waking hour down at the bay, getting the dilapidated building ready for its customers. He had thought of little else. "Effie told you about my conversation with Madame Odette, I presume?"

Rosy carefully explained the plan she had formulated with the ballet teacher, how she would attend a riding lesson only once a month, but still keep her job at Allaway Farm Stables to earn the money for her lessons.

"Won't it be hard for you, Rosy, to be around the horses knowing that you could not ride them as much as you would like to?" questioned Tom.

"I'll manage," replied Rosy, her stubborn streak quickly surfacing. "I want to help you."

"You're a generous girl Rosy," smiled Tom, hugging his niece. "In a way I'm grateful for this war. It brought you to this village, to Ivy House, and I wouldn't change a thing." Rosy grinned, climbing slowly up the stairs until she reached the first floor landing where she turned around with a cheeky grin.

"Why don't you invite Evelyn as your date to

the Ceilidh on Saturday after the show?" she suggested, giggling as Tom blushed a delicate pink. "See you in the morning!"

Chapter Twelve
STAGE STRUCK

As Rosy waited in the wings with a fluttering stomach, she caught her best friend's eye from the other side of the church hall stage and smiled excitedly. She could hear her heart beating loudly, the rhythmic thumping becoming almost hypnotic as Rosy became zoned-in to her character. She stood half aware of the bustling around her, doing little exercises to warm up the tense muscles in her feet.

As the final minutes before curtain-up elapsed, the eager chatter of the cast faded into anxious whispers and frenzied costume-checks. Rosy straightened her green felt tunic and pulled up her tights before making sure her ballet shoe ribbons were done up correctly. What if they came undone during the show? Rosy dared not think about that. Instead, she concentrated on her breathing, and began to relax.

The bee-like hum of the audience's murmurs grew louder as more people filed expectantly into their seats. Mothers, fathers, grandparents and siblings all crowded into the cramped space to enjoy the afternoon's entertainment that 'Robin Hood: a

Swashbuckling Ballet', was soon to provide.

Rosy's meditation was broken by her friend Logan's exclamation of "Rosy! Have you seen your family yet? I've found where they're sitting."

She lead Rosy onto the stage towards a tiny gap in the curtains. "They're next to Audrey's family, behind my grandma," she explained, letting Rosy have her turn at looking. Rosy quickly and nervously scanned the rows of people, paranoid that someone might see her.

Her heart leapt when she noticed Tom deep in animated conversation with Audrey's father. Next to them were Evelyn and Mrs. McGregor who were proudly reading the small paper programmes. Rosy smiled as Evelyn beamed and pointed to what she presumed was her sister's name inside.

"Five minutes please!" came a shout from Madame Odette's husband at the back of the hall, whereupon Logan yelped and clung to Rosy's arm.

"Five minutes! I can't do this Rosy!" Rosy squeezed the quivering girl's hand and led her back to the stage-left wing, where she whispered, somewhat surprised by her confident words,

"You will be absolutely fine, just enjoy it." She smoothed down Logan's elegant powder blue velvet dress, a tiny bit of jealousy surfacing as she looked down at her own masculine costume.

"And besides, you'll make the prettiest court lady they've ever seen!" she added, feeling her spirits rise as Logan nodded, and grinned bravely.

"Thank you Rosy," she sighed. "I wish I were as confident as you." At that moment there was a sudden hush as the hall lights were faded down and the first few notes of the overture started, struck up by Alistair on the old wooden piano.

Rosy's heart stopped for a few seconds. This was it! The last sudden panic about costume and props came, followed by a brief, terrified notion from everyone that they had all forgotten every step, and then, the soft fateful cry of "curtain up!" from backstage.

The moth-eaten burgundy curtains swished slowly apart, revealing the beautifully painted backdrop of a forest scene. This had been enthusiastically produced by Tom who had agreed to paint all the backdrops for the show in return for a free ticket. Evelyn elbowed him excitedly as she saw the splendour of the stage and playfully whispered, "so that's why the café has taken so long to prepare. Those trees must have taken you a very long time!"

A few seconds later, Rosy noticed her cue in the music, and her friends squealed a final "break a leg!" before she found herself centre stage, gazing dazedly out at the sea of upturned heads before her. For what seemed like minutes, but was actually only a couple of seconds, she just stood there, her heart thumping like a caged animal in her chest, the feeling of expectation buzzing in the air.

Spectacles gleamed, the footlights dazzled, and the entire cast held their breath as their leading dancer's eyes flitted from side to side, desperately trying to spot a familiar face.

With a sigh of relief, she met the gaze of old Mrs. McGregor, who nodded her head in encouragement. The music stopped, ready for Robin Hood to begin the first solo; Rosy's eyes glinted as she soaked up the atmosphere, finding that it fuelled her, giving her such an incredible energy that when she started to leap round the stage she felt as if she were flying.

For the next minute she was a daring, heroic outlaw, and as the other cast members joined her on the stage, her fiery attitude was infectious. Everyone danced better than they had ever danced before. Confidence grew, and by the time Rosy had to join with Audrey for their final pas de deux, the audience and dancers were very content.

Stewart Murdoch, a tall, handsome boy of age fifteen (and the object of Audrey's great interest) played the part of Lady Marion's lady in waiting with such hilarity, dressed rather fetchingly in a huge puffy dress and pink satin ballet slippers. After his solo at the end of Act One the applause was magnificent, and many people had tears of laughter running down their cheeks, much to his delight.

There had only been one minor hiccup when

one of the tiny little girls in the adorable dance of the woodland flowers declared that she needed to go to the toilet right in the middle of the scene. Luckily, the audience found this extremely cute, and one of the Merry Men led the confused tot off, trying desperately to conceal his giggles.

When the last few steps of the finale number had been executed by the elated, if a little tired, cast, Rosy and Audrey glanced at each other with huge grins across their faces. Alistair played the final chord and the audience broke out into thunderous applause, which echoed around the confined space and rang like music in Rosy's ears.

"I think they liked it!" she gasped, beaming at Tom, whose hands were clapping perhaps most earnestly of all. "My, that was fun." As she stepped forward to receive her curtain call, Rosy was on top of the world. She savoured every second, curtsying deeply and gesturing to Alistair to stand up. He did so, bowing to another wave of applause.

The curtain fell on the company of young performers and the audience began to leave the hall, chattering intently on every aspect of the show. Backstage in the dressing rooms it was a flurry of relieved laughter and tiredness, and fifteen minutes later Rosy and Audrey stepped gratefully out into the frosty air where they were met by Tom, Mrs. McGregor, Evelyn and Mr. Price, who gave their congratulations in turn.

The party hurried back to Ivy House, where Mrs. McGregor started immediately on the dinner, and the adults settled down in front of the fire to talk. The two girls raced up to Rosy's attic bedroom where they took the numerous pins out of their buns and began to remove the last of their thick stage makeup.

"I'm nearly out of cold cream!" moaned Audrey, tipping her pot upside down and nicking some of Rosy's, grimacing as the cool lotion touched her still hot skin. "I hate stage lights, they make me so boiling."

"I don't!" protested Rosy, combing her fingers through her mass of hair and spinning happily round the room. "I love being under the lights."

Audrey giggled, "You've only been on a stage once and suddenly you've gone all stage struck!"

"Well, maybe I am," said Rosy, her eyes bright and wistful. "Oh, Audrey, I'm going to be on the stage for a career if it's the last thing I do!"

***

A few hours later, Rosy and Audrey joined what looked like the entire village in squeezing into Tom's new 'Ivy Café' for the traditional Christmas Ceilidh. This was the first time the café had been opened and so far the evening had been a success.

The event involved lots of music and dancing

and general merriment; Rosy was enjoying herself immensely. It was her first experience of a real Scottish celebration so it was all very new to her, but the villagers had been more than keen to teach her all the dances and explain the strange rituals.

A group of rowdy village men had agreed to play their fiddles and accordions for the dances after being bribed with free drinks, and Audrey had offered to hand round nibbles. The atmosphere was wonderful. Everyone had rosy cheeks and smiles on their faces.

Tom was in his element as he had taken the opportunity to make a bit of money. He was behind the counter selling food and drinks and other festive items such as pots of Mrs. McGregor's homemade cranberry jelly, holly wreaths and mistletoe from the trees at the campsite.

"Doesn't the place look good!" he grinned at Rosy while generously pouring out glasses of home-brewed beer. The building did indeed look very smart, and the small group who had helped to renovate it were very proud of themselves.

The walls had been painted a cosy green, mistletoe had been hung from every rafter, and framed paintings of Tom's were hanging for sale on the wall. Tom had decided not to put the tables out yet, as a ceilidh demands a lot of space for the various reels and two-steps.

"Mince pie?" offered Audrey, sitting down

heavily in the chair next to Rosy, joining in to watch the dancing for a few minutes. She soon jumped to her feet again, clutching the tray to her chest for fear of it being knocked from her hands by a tipsy reveller.

"I'll do that if you like," offered Rosy, getting to her feet and attempting to pull the tray from Audrey's adamant grasp. "You go and join in the next dance."

"What is it?" asked Audrey.

"Something called Strip the Willow?" ventured Rosy, shrugging her shoulders. "These dances all have such funny names, I can't make head nor tail of it."

Audrey shoved her friend back down onto her chair. "You just sit there and enjoy yourself," she demanded. "I've danced that one hundreds of times before!" She tucked an unruly lock of fair hair behind her ear thoughtfully. "But I'll do the Circassian Circle with you later, that's always great fun. Call me when it's time, but in the mean time relax!"

Rosy watched her disappear into the throng and sat back, observing the villagers wind in and out of each other, their colourful shapes eventually blurring into one as the music became faster and louder.

She looked around the room for someone she knew to talk to, and spotted her uncle and Evelyn in the far corner. They had become very close over the last months, and the girls had noticed the chemistry between them: the way Evelyn's eyes sparkled when they talked, and the way that Tom became all flustered whenever her name was mentioned.

Rosy watched them laugh together for a while, and she was just about to go over and join in their conversation when Tom looked up and noticed a sprig of mistletoe directly above him. Evelyn smiled shyly as their heads drew closer, until their lips gently met, and Rosy's jaw dropped.

She had to find Audrey, quickly! She eventually found her helping Mrs. McGregor to make another batch of mince pies in the poky kitchen at the back of the building.

"You will never guess what I have just witnessed," she blurted out, jumping around in excitement and making a mind-blowingly tartan clad Mrs. McGregor drop her rolling pin into the bowl next to her.

"Whatever it is, I am pretty sure it's not that ground-breaking," she gasped, desperately trying to retrieve the rolling pin without getting mincemeat everywhere.

"Oh it definitely is!"

"What is it Rosy? Do tell," whined Audrey.

"I just saw Tom and your sister *kissing!*" exclaimed Rosy, causing the poor old lady to drop her rolling pin again.

"What!" screamed Audrey. "How exciting!" Mrs. McGregor gave up with the mince pies to stare narrow-eyed at Rosy.

"Are you quite sure?" she asked.

"Of course I'm sure."

"But he's too old for her!" Rosy and Audrey grinned at each other,

"He's only thirty five."

"Yes and she's twenty one," squeaked the baffled housekeeper, "practically a bairn!"

"That doesn't matter," laughed Audrey. "I'll be Rosy's half aunt!"

"What, when?" asked Mrs. McGregor.

"When Tom and Eve get married of course."

"Gosh! That's peculiar," giggled Rosy. Mrs. McGregor shook her head in amusement,

"Now that's what I call jumping to a conclusion."

Chapter Thirteen
THE HIGHLAND GAMES

As the few weeks after Christmas Eve swiftly passed, business at Ivy Café was going superbly. Interest in the venture had risen, especially with the people who had been staying in the area over the Christmas holiday period. These visitors were mostly from towns and therefore found the rugged landscapes and rural scenery extremely fascinating and quaint. Many of them bought Tom's paintings to take home as a memory of their time in the village.

So overall things were going well for Tom and the others, and especially for Rosy. Her recent success in Robin Hood had improved her confidence greatly, and now not a single doubt was in her mind about a career in dance. She was still working at the stables to pay for her ballet lessons, and that also made her feel very independent and very grown up.

Rosy was a kind-hearted girl and took great pleasure in helping other people, so giving up her free time to labour at Allaway Farm in order to assist her uncle was no chore to her. Tom could see this, and was very proud of his niece, as were

Rosy's parents who had received a letter from him telling of their daughter's generosity.

At first Rosy thought that it would be extremely hard for her to be around the horses so much while knowing that she would hardly be able to ride them at all for fear of ruining her chances of being a ballet dancer. However, she was increasingly finding herself able to dwell on all the good things that she had in her life, instead of on what she was not able to do.

Rosy had a loving family, a group of fabulous friends and an amazing talent, and she soon found that by appreciating these things the bad aspects of her life didn't seem quite so bad after all. A small bit of her schoolwork, however, had been suffering due to her intense concentration on ballet. She had lately been struggling slightly with her mathematics, and being such a determined person it was potentially easy for her to become stressed and anxious about it.

But she was also a very intelligent and resourceful young girl, and decided to enlist the help of Faye Morrison who was more than happy to assist. Faye was an excellent mathematician. Giving Rosy some after-school tuition proved to help her understanding as well, and it also provided the friends with an excuse to meet up and have a gossip more often!

So once she had got her academic progress

back on track Rosy really had nothing to worry about, except for the fact that she hadn't heard from her mother for several weeks.

This didn't really bother her too much as she knew that things were hard back in London, what with the more frequent air raids that were happening now. There was also the fact that her mother had been enlisted to work in a factory to make ammunition. It was likely that she hadn't had the time to write a letter. Rosy dared not think about any other reason behind the lack of communication.

Like everyone else she had learnt to be optimistic and always to hope for the best. After all there was no other way the country would be able to survive the war; no one knew how long it would last, how many casualties there would be and when the brave soldiers would return home to their families.

So Rosy gritted her teeth and completely absorbed herself in her dancing, trying not to think of the inevitable suffering that her mother was going through so many miles away.

There were other things beside her ballet training and work at the stables to take Rosy's mind off the war. Very soon, there was to be a 'Highland Games' in the village. Usually this event would take place in the height of summer, however the organiser's son was due to be leaving for the army in March so it was decided that it would be held early in the year. Unconventional plans such as this were not uncommon in the village – they certainly had strange ways of going about things.

Rosy and Audrey were going to do a display of Highland dancing for the visitors. The event was to take place at the campsite, and preparations were in full swing. Each year previously tourists had flocked to see the traditional events such as races, bagpipe competitions and caber tossing, and Tom wasn't taking any chances with the arrangements. Ration coupons had been saved for extra food to sell, and everything had been given a new lick of paint to make the place look as presentable as possible.

The days before the games crept past, and before they knew it Rosy and Audrey had only twenty-four more hours to make their performance perfect. As part of dance classes with Madame Odette, all pupils were taught basic Highland dances, although Audrey had been doing it ever since she was a tiny little girl. In that respect she had a steep advantage, but Rosy was a quick learner and soon picked up the steps to all the well known dances.

On the evening before the games the two girls were up at Allaway Farm deciding on their costumes. "We want to go for something as traditional as possible," decided Audrey, rummaging through her wardrobe until she felt her fingers brush against something smooth at the very back. "Aha!" she cried, extracting a vivid red velvety bodice with gold trimmings around the sleeves and shiny gold buttons down the front. "This ought to fit you."

"What is it?" asked Rosy, gingerly reaching for it and holding it up against her.

"It goes on top of a blouse," replied a muffled voice, and Audrey's top half emerged from the wardrobe holding a frilly white blouse with frothy white lace at the neck. Rosy giggled. "I'll look like a sheep wearing that!" she exclaimed, indignantly.

"You wait until you see the kilt!" came the amused retort.

Several minutes later the girls were finally kitted out in full highland dress, and they did look the part. Audrey was wearing a pretty white dress with a purple tartan sash across the back and Rosy had eventually resigned herself to being put in a kilt and bodice. And actually, now she had seen her reflection, she didn't think it so bad at all.

"What fun!" she grinned, standing in first position in front of Audrey's full-length mirror. "It's just like dressing up. I've never worn a real kilt before."

They had a final practise of their dances, then Rosy looked at the clock and yelped. "Heavens! The time! Tom will be here to pick me up any minute now". The girls hastily got back into their day clothes and ran downstairs. They found Mr. Price and Evelyn in the kitchen, where Evelyn gestured to the chairs opposite her and asked,

"So girls, do you feel ready for tomorrow?"

"I think so," nodded Rosy, "but I'm still petrified!" Evelyn frowned in disbelief,

"What, you? Never."

"It just feels so strange to me," said Rosy. "I'm really scared I'll let you down Audrey." Audrey gave her best friend a hug and sighed.

"Oh Rosy, whatever will we do with you. You manage to step out on a stage and lead a show, but as soon as you're faced with performing a few silly dances to a few silly visitors you've turned all insecure on me."

Rosy laughed gratefully and nodded, "I know, I'll be fine, it's just I've never done anything like this before." Her eyes gleamed as she thought of performing again so soon. "I can't wait!" Just then the doorbell sounded and Evelyn leapt to her feet.

"That'll be Tom, I'll go and see him in." Rosy and Audrey exchanged knowing glances as the young lady checked her lipstick and hurried off to the front door.

She returned a few seconds later followed by Tom, who shook her father's hand warmly. "Thank you for having Rosy again Mr. Price."

"No it's a pleasure, I haven't heard a peep from the two all afternoon. They've been hard at work practising for the games tomorrow." Evelyn smiled, and murmured hopefully,

"Are you sure you won't stay for a spot of tea Tom?"

"Thank you, but no. I still have things to do at the campsite." Evelyn raised her eyebrows.

"At eight o'clock at night?"

"I had a disaster with some bunting and some sheep, no time to explain - Effie should have rustled something up for when I get home."

At that, he repeated his thanks and ushered Rosy out of the door into the dark farmyard. The only sound to be heard was the gabbling of the geese by the pond and the occasional dog's bark. It was a beautiful evening. "At least there's no chance of rain tomorrow!" he rejoiced as they walked briskly down the lane towards the campsite. "A rainy highland games would be a nightmare."

***

Tom glared in annoyance out of the kitchen window onto the saturated campsite field and sodden awnings. Sleet pelted diagonally across the slate-grey sky down onto the dishevelled scene below and dense clouds blocked out any trace of sunlight.

"I told you it wouldn't rain," he sighed resentfully, checking the clock and making his way towards the door. Rosy sat in the corner in her nicely ironed costume massaging her feet, staring at her uncle in his shorts and vest with amusement.

"You are going to be freezing!" she giggled. "At least Audrey and I are dancing inside in the barn today."

Tom was to compete in the running races, hence his unusual attire, and was not looking forward to it. "At least I'm making money from all the visitors," he contemplated, grabbing his mackintosh and flinging one at Rosy.

He took her hand, finding that it was very slightly shaking. "You're not nervous are you?" he said.

"A bit," she replied, jumping up and down on the spot to keep warm. "What if I mess up? Then I've let Audrey down."

Tom sighed, shoving her out of the door into the front garden. "Don't be silly, most of the people watching won't know the difference if you go wrong. I know *I* won't! Besides, I doubt anyone else will have turned up anyway."

Grimacing as the icy sleet spattered onto their faces, the two made their way across the squelchy grass towards the barn. The building was seldom ever used, and then only for activities such as indoor cricket and the like - but now it was a hive of activity.

Despite the poor weather conditions the whole

village had turned up for a day of fun and competition, which was getting off to a good start. Tom and Rosy had heard the instantly recognisable drone of bagpipes right from the other side of the campsite, and when they heaved open the heavy wooden doors the piercing sound hit them and almost knocked them off their feet.

Rosy looked around with wide eyes. She thought she had taken in sufficient Scottish culture at the Christmas Ceilidh, but this was something else!

The overwhelming clash of tartans was amazing for a start and it took a long time for Rosy's eyes to become used to it. An array of multi-coloured bunting hung like spiders webs from the rafters, adding to the blast of colour.

People were in various states of traditional dress, ranging from the sports competitors in thin white vests and navy shorts, to pipers in full national costume with socks, sporrans and all, to the conspicuous visitors who had turned up in their drab-by-comparison daywear.

Rosy could pick up snippets of individual conversations from the loudest and most broadly Scottish of the crowd and was relieved to find Audrey running up to her, grinning hugely. As soon as the games had been declared open, Rosy and Audrey were called onto the makeshift stage of upturned grocery crates to perform their dances.

It went extremely well, and once the first few hard dances were over Rosy began to relax and enjoy herself, especially the rare experience of being able to perform traditional Highland dancing with the accompaniment of a genuine Scottish bagpiper.

They took their bows together when they had finished and raced off panting to remove the tight black shoes which were beginning to constrict the blood flow to their feet.

As Audrey unwound the long laces from around her instep she grinned and looked up at her friend. "How cultured are *you*!" she laughed. "A ceilidh and a Highland Games all in under two months. I would almost forget you weren't Scottish if it wasn't for your frightful English accent!"

Rosy giggled and pulled a face. Audrey gave her best friend a hug and sighed contentedly. "I do love events like these!" she cried. "Even in the middle of a war, everyone is having so much fun, it makes you proud to be Scottish!"

Chapter Fourteen
MISSING

As the weather turned from sleet to snow the spirit of the people was not dampened. Everybody made their way outside onto the field, their impressive costumes now unfortunately covered with heavy black raincoats and layers of extra clothing ready for the main events to begin.

The unmistakable sound of bagpipes continued to float across the village as the men got on with competitions such as caber-tossing, shot put and running races. The women amused themselves watching and staffing the numerous stalls that lined the edges of the field.

Rosy won a bar of chocolate on the tombola, a luxury that was rare due to the heavy rationing restrictions that were now in place. She sat down under a tree to share it with Audrey and Evelyn, and watched the snow falling with satisfaction.

Evelyn seemed to share her thoughts as she remarked, "Why have a warm Highland Games when you can have one in the snow? This is much more imaginative."

She blissfully swallowed her mouthful of chocolate and added, "And I do enjoy watching the men pretending not to be cold in their sports vests!"

In the afternoon Tom came second in three of his races and third in the hurdles. He was very pleased with himself. He came stumbling over to the girls and hugged the three of them in turn. "My, I haven't done that much exercise since I was a boy!" he gasped, gratefully receiving the thick sheepskin coat which Evelyn had brought for him to wear.

Rosy noticed that he was shaking from head to foot, but put it down to the freezing weather conditions and the exhaustion from having run so far. He then disappeared into the crowd to talk to his friends leaving Rosy, Audrey and Evelyn to enjoy the variety of entertainment that there was on offer.

They entered into the 'guess the weight of the haggis' competition and bought scarves made from local sheep's wool: a yellow one for Audrey, blue for Rosy and green for Evelyn to match her beautiful eyes. Rosy's favourite activity of the day was the 'welly wanging' which involved flinging a wellington boot backwards over your head as far as you could!

An hour later it began to get dark and still the snow fell onto the hardened ground, slowly concealing the battered turf and turning it from brown to a crisp white. Contented visitors began to disperse until there were only a few people left in the barn, all sitting at the high table drinking beer and discussing the day's events. Rosy and Audrey sat next to Evelyn, trying to engage her in conversation but failing; the young woman was staring in concern out of the window.

She had not seen Tom since he had finished his races, and as the dark drew in she became steadily more anxious as to his whereabouts. "He's probably at the house getting warm," Rosy reassured her.

However when a worried Mrs. McGregor appeared at the door in her coat and boots from the house asking if they had seen him, her suspicions were confirmed and she immediately ran from the barn into the bitter evening.

There was an ancient gate that stood on the perimeter of the campsite. It opened into a small, dense hazel wood, where Tom often went with Evelyn to draw or simply to stroll and take in the musky smell of the nuts on the branches. When Evelyn reached it she paused before gingerly pushing it open, hardly able to see now as darkness fell.

She strained her eyes to make out the footpath, not caring about the overgrown ferns that brushed against her legs, snagging her woollen stockings. Just as she was becoming desperate she noticed a dark shape on the damp ground at her feet.

With a shriek she realised that it was the man she'd been searching for, and within seconds some people came to her aid. They carried Tom to Ivy House and laid him on the sofa. Luckily the village doctor, who had only just left the event, was called for and in very little time had managed to rouse the ice cold man, praising Evelyn for her efforts and placing Tom's care in her capable and willing hands.

***

The next day Tom had fully regained consciousness. It was decided that his weak heart, the reason for him not joining the army, was to blame for his collapse. The snowy conditions and a sudden burst of exercise on his part had triggered it, and if it hadn't been for Evelyn's quick thinking he would almost certainly have died of hypothermia.

The doctor prescribed a good rest and forbade the shaken Tom to walk or do anything that involved sudden or rough movement.

An anxious Evelyn took a few weeks off her horse riding instructing and competing in order to tend to her beloved Tom's every need. He was extensively grateful and never tired of telling her how eternally indebted he was, and how he was so lucky to have met her.

She didn't mind caring for him a bit. Neither did Rosy mind about Evelyn's constant company at Ivy House. She was almost like a big sister to the young girl and never tired to chat with her or watch her dance. It seemed so normal to have a bright and breezy Evelyn in the house now.

More of Evelyn meant Rosy could see much more of Audrey too. Their friendship became even stronger and more unbreakable, a bond that they would have for the rest of their lives, everyone was certain. And for Rosy's thirteenth birthday Audrey organised a surprise party at the farm to which all their friends were invited. That spring turned out to be the one of the best times of her life.

Gradually Tom regained his strength and by summer he was almost fully back to normal, although still not permitted to do anything at all too strenuous.

Rosy, on the other hand, threw herself into a new term of ballet lessons with great vigour and soon grew from being a good dancer to an exceptional one. Madame Odette nurtured her star student and encouraged her unfailingly towards her goal of becoming a ballet dancer. The other students soon gave up trying to keep pace with the talented Rosy.

Chapter Fifteen
POINTE SHOE DAY

The day that Rosy had been waiting for for years started crisp and bright, and as she skipped down the hill towards the church hall, her ballet bag swinging to and fro from her shoulder, she felt as light as air. Today was the day that Madame Odette would tell the girls if they were ready to advance on to pointe, and Rosy couldn't wait.

From that very first Christmas Day when she received her dancing shoes, tutu and now rather-dog eared little ballet book, Rosy had sat and stared in admiration at the illustrations of older girls balancing effortlessly on the tips of their toes, wishing that she could be allowed a pair of pointe shoes of her own.

It takes years of training to be strong enough to acomplish the steps and support oneself from the ankles, however Madame Odette had decided that Rosy had worked hard enough over the last few years to be safely considered for the shoes.

When they had arrived at the hall and excitedly changed into their practise dresses, Madame Odette sat the girls down on the floor and began the process of checking that their feet were strong and developed enough. It felt like such a technical procedure, and Rosy's patience would have got the better of her if she had not been as sensible as she was and realised that it was for all of their safety.

While she was waiting she sat and gazed at Audrey's feet, which she had always envied. They had beautiful high arches that she knew would look just divine in pointe shoes. Audrey had the perfect feet for a dancer, but just didn't want to go into the profession. She wanted to be a nurse which frustrated Rosy greatly as she had only average feet and considered it very hard luck.

Madame Odette proceeded down the line of students making them point their toes and then seeing if they could rise onto demi-pointe with no assistance and stay there for a number of seconds. Rosy passed these tests with ease and the entire class was told that they were to go to Edinburgh and purchase a pair of their own pointe shoes before the month was out.

A few weeks before, Rosy had written to her mother to tell her of the news that she would soon become a fully fledged ballerina. Her mother had sent back an envelope with enough money to buy her the shoes, and a note in which she said that she had been saving for months in order for Rosy to have them.

So as soon as she got back to Ivy House, Rosy sprinted up to her room and retrieved the envelope from the dressing table drawer with an excited squeal. She ran down the stairs to the kitchen only to find Evelyn sitting at the table thoughtfully sipping an almost empty cup of tea and twiddling a gleaming lock of hair around her finger.

She looked up and gave a gentle smile as Rosy crept enquiringly through the door. "I'm afraid Tom's had to go to London," she said. Rosy frowned.

"To London? What ever for?" Evelyn shrugged her shoulders.

"I have no idea, he just pulled me close and asked me to go with you, Audrey and Mrs. McGregor to Edinburgh tomorrow in his stead to get you your pointe shoes. He'll be back as soon as he can."

She stood up, placed her cup in the sink and hugged Rosy tightly. "I'm sure it is nothing to worry about, Mrs. McGregor will be here tonight. Are you sure you'll be alright?"

Rosy buried her head in the soft fabric of Evelyn's cardigan, deeply inhaling her flowery perfume. The scent calmed her instantly. Evelyn tenderly ruffled Rosy's hair and ushered her back up the stairs with her envelope of money.

"Now you just look forward to tomorrow, I know it's a big deal for you." She grabbed her bag and opened the door. "Try and get some sleep won't you?" she begged, feeling greatly responsible for the young girl now the master of the house was away. "Although if you're anything as excited as Audrey is then that may be quite difficult!" With one last pondering glance at the briefcase that Tom had left in the kitchen in his rush to get away, she swept out of the door.

Rosy was immensely cheered by the reminder of her new pointe shoes and jogged happily up the stairs to her bedroom. Soon she would know what being 'en pointe' felt like, and she just couldn't contain her excitement.

***

The next day, or 'pointe shoe day' as Rosy and Audrey liked to call it, was a Friday, the day Rosy always received the weekly letters from her mother. She had not had one the week before, but that didn't worry her as she knew that because of the war communication could be quite unpredictable.

Today, however, when she ran eagerly to the front door mat only to find a few bills for her uncle, she began to think the situation quite odd. She trudged into the kitchen and gave the bills to Mrs. McGregor who frowned and placed them on the already growing pile of things for Tom to sort out when he returned from London.

"Any news from Tom?" she inquired, prodding at the bowl of porridge that was placed in front of her with her spoon, a complicated mixture of anxiety and excitement destroying her appetite.

The old housekeeper shook her head. "I'm afraid not," she replied. "I do wish I knew what was going on."

Whisking the uneaten bowl of porridge from beneath Rosy's nose without really thinking she pulled Rosy upright and lead her into the hallway. She straightened the increasingly impatient girl's collar and checked that her plaits were neat. Finally, when content with Rosy's smartness, she hurried her out of the door.

When they arrived at Allaway farm an equally excited Audrey jumped into the back of the car with Rosy. Evelyn, dressed in her smart 'going into town' outfit, climbed into the front seat next to Mrs. McGregor and they made the short journey to the train station, which involved a hair-raisingly narrow mountain track and numerous encounters with death-defying sheep.

While the adults chatted about Tom's various traits, the two girls kept themselves amused with a game of 'I Spy'. This, however, soon became boring as their vocabulary was limited to "Sheep" or "Tree" or "Rock".

On the train they then spent half an hour singing songs at the tops of their voices until they were quelled by a penetrating look from Mrs. McGregor. So they spent the rest of the journey speaking only in French, which Audrey was exceptionally good at, and eventually arrived at the bustling town with much relief from the adults. Mrs. McGregor rushed off to buy provisions, leaving Evelyn in charge of the two highly impatient girls who wanted nothing more than to go straight to the dance shop.

The three made their way down the busy streets, gazing in wonder at the rainbow array of shops as they passed. It was the first time that Rosy had been in a town since leaving London and her parents. As they hurried along with Evelyn's heels clicking loudly on the stone pavements, she wondered if everything was alright so many miles away.

She was startled when they came to a stop outside a tiny green-fronted shop with its paintwork in a very sorry state. Rosy tried to peer through the grimy windows, but with not much success as the interior of the shop was too dark and the glass too old for her to see anything at all.

A small handpainted sign hung above the wonky purple door that read "Mrs. Swan's Dance Store – Suppliers of finest quality dance wear since 1900".

Audrey grinned. "Well, this is it. We always come here to buy our dance things." Evelyn smirked when she noticed Rosy reading the sign.

"I don't know about 'finest quality' but it's the

best we are going to be getting for our coupons!"
She pushed open the door and walked into the store,
and with rapidly beating hearts Rosy and Audrey
followed. It was an Aladdin's cave of intriguing
objects with an authentic musty smell and cosy dim
lighting from several antique oil lamps to make up
for the lack of sunlight from the dusty windows.

Rosy looked around her at the fascinating
jumble of costumes, shoes and bags. Three of the
walls were covered in glass-fronted cabinets with
separate drawers for different kinds of leotard,
tights and various other items of clothing. Close to
the ceiling sat rows and rows of tutu skirts, their
richly coloured layers of netting blooming like
strange flowers from the tops of the cabinets.

When Rosy noticed an entire wall of shelving
packed to bursting with shiny new ballet shoes
something inside her leapt in exhilaration. She saw
the rows of pink satin pointe shoes sitting there
gleaming invitingly, and grabbed Audrey's hand.
"We're getting pointe shoes!" she squealed, her
cheeks shining a deep pink as a result of a mixture
of the heat of the room and enthusiasm.

"Honestly girls," sighed Evelyn. "The way you
two get het up about it, it's like we've won the war
already." At the sound of her silvery voice a weasel-
like bright auburn-haired lady appeared from behind
a pile of tutus and squinted at them through a pair of
very thick horn-rimmed glasses.

"Goodness gracious, if it isn't the Price sisters!" she croaked, peering at Evelyn curiously. "My, haven't you grown Audrey!" A bemused Evelyn cleared her throat.

"I'm Evelyn, Mary, *this* is my sister Audrey." Mary, for that was the name of the batty shop keeper, shook her head in amazement.

"Ah yes, I remember now. I haven't seen young Audrey since she was a wee lassy."

She turned her attention back to Evelyn who was beginning to become impatient with this kind-hearted, but very elderly woman. "Now you must be, what, eighteen now, Evelyn?" she squinted.

"I'm twenty two," came the disgruntled reply.

A long conversation ensued, consisting mainly of "Haven't you grown?" and "My eyesight's not as good as it used to be...". They finally got down to the pointe shoe fitting just as the three customers were losing the will to live.

Rosy padded her toes with lambs wool and slipped her feet into the first pair of firm satin slippers. As soon as the ribbons were safely hugging her ankles, the cheer was back and she threw herself wholeheartedly into trying on a variety of different models of pointe shoe.

Audrey, however, was a slightly more difficult customer than her friend, as her beautiful high arches meant that she had to have special hard soled shoes to support her feet. Whenever she thought she had chosen a comfortable pair, Mary raised a shaking finger and declared, "The shoe chooses the dancer my dear!"

At the end of the hour both girls were exhausted but still excited about clutching their gorgeous new shoes while Evelyn sorted out the payment. They left the shop leaving piles of shoes for the poor doddery Mary to sort out.

When they stepped out of the poky shop into the clear fresh air, Evelyn sighed deeply and smiled. "Ah! I can breathe again. If I had stayed one more minute in that stuffy place, I swear I would have passed out!"

Rosy grinned. "I think it's an absolute jem of a shop, but what I don't understand is how that Mary woman can manage to tell exactly what shoes give the perfect line if she can't even tell you two apart."

Evelyn took the girls' hands. "Now *that* no one could ever tell you, but Mary fitted my pointe shoes years ago. It's an art!"

"You sound so learned, O wise one," teased Audrey before dragging her sister down the road towards the station where Mrs. McGregor was waiting for them.

***

Rosy and Audrey spent the whole evening in the disused dining room at Ivy House, clomping about in the noisy shoes and trying to balance on the tips of their toes without their ankles bending over into all sorts of awkward positions. It must be said that Rosy was more sensible in this matter than her best friend, and was content with rising up and down, enjoying the exhilarating feeling that being 'en pointe' gave her.

Audrey, however, was intent on trying arabesques and pirouettes and all manner of advanced steps, and no matter how much Rosy nagged her she carried on anyway and by the end of the evening was covered in bruises and blisters.

Both of their bottoms had made contact with the hard wooden floor several times as the tips of their shoes were still shiny satin and would continue to be slippery until the girls got round to darning them: a very long and painful task.

Rosy loved the feeling of wearing her shoes so much that she crept into bed with them still on, although she couldn't feel her feet in the morning!

By Monday, both the girls had not stopped dancing and although their feet were now unrecognisable their technique had become stronger. Madame Odette was very impressed at their 'natural' talent at pointe work (the two met eyes and decided not to tell her that they had in fact spent the whole weekend practising).

Rosy came out of the class happier than she had been in her life. But when she got home her mood swung instantly. She let herself in through the door to find Mrs. McGregor comforting a sobbing Tom on the sofa in the living room. She rushed in in a panic, and was immediately pulled into the huddle.

"Rosy," soothed the housekeeper taking a deep breath. "Your father's been killed fighting in France."

Chapter Sixteen
EVELYN COMES INTO HER OWN

Now Rosy knew the extent of Audrey's heartbreak when her mother had passed away. Any feeling of annoyance at her best friend not having told her about it, however minutely small, had disappeared, and she was suddenly overwhelmed with a desire to see Audrey, to hug her tightly and talk about these emotions that felt as though they were drowning her.

But it was so hard to talk about it, even to the people closest to her. Even to Audrey, Evelyn or Mrs. McGregor. However it was especially hard to talk to her Uncle Tom, her father's little brother. In the days following the news of his brother's death Tom had become almost unbearable to be around.

He didn't really eat anything and whenever anybody said something he just snapped back in response. He left his curly mop of hair to become tangled and even more unruly.

He completely retreated inside himself and rather selfishly left Mrs. McGregor to deal with running the campsite while he wasted away in the living room, staring out of the window as the green foliage of summer turned to amber and the leaves began to flutter from the branches and settle on the unmown lawn.

This was Tom's favourite time of year, especially as an artist. He usually marvelled at the vivid colours in the landscape and took long walks with friends through the heather and trees, stopping frequently to sketch the detailed pattern of a fallen leaf or to draw the village children collecting conkers. But this year was different.

Eventually he stopped crying, only now he sat with a set face, an almost resentful expression. When Evelyn managed, once, to talk to him, she discovered that he was feeling guilty for not seeing his brother and his family enough.

Years ago he had rushed straight from London to buy the campsite and only got to see Rosy's father briefly on special occasions. Apart from that she could get no further coherent sentences from him and decided to leave him alone for a while.

Rosy could not bear to be in this dark environment, and she sought release by being outside, playing ball with the small children or sitting and talking with the wives as they sat on the walls in front of their cottages. As she got to know the villagers better, she realised that many families were fatherless because of the war, and this made her feel much less alone.

There was one visitor to the campsite that Rosy had befriended, a Mr. Sayers, whom she found out owned a prestigious drama school in London. She sat for hours listening to him tell tales of his life in the theatre.

He was very interested to hear of her ambitions to go into the theatre herself, and although he did not know much about dance, he gave her many useful tips on stagecraft which she treasured. When she was with him she could forget about the tragedies of her life and lose herself in her dreams of becoming a professional ballet dancer, her only real hope at the moment.

A month after her father's death Rosy received an envelope from her mother which contained a bracelet in a small velvet box. She watched the light glinting off the polished coloured beads, pondering the meaning of this unexpected gift. Putting the box into her dressing table drawer she began to read the accompanying letter, letting it float to the ground as she sank onto her bed in shock.

Her mother had written to tell her that she had met an American Airforce pilot, Simon, at a dance and she felt that her daughter ought to know this news first. She still 'missed her late husband greatly', but found that 'when she was with Simon everything seemed so much brighter', and she knew that Rosy's father would want her to be happy.

Rosy, however, was definately not happy. She yelled out at the piece of crumpled paper and stuffed it forcefully, along with the precious locket which she had worn everyday since being evacuated, into the drawer. "How dare she? How dare she?" she sobbed, pummelling her pillow with her fists, seething. Mrs. McGregor burst through the door upon hearing her cries and pulled a struggling Rosy next to her.

"What's happened Rosy?" she coaxed, but the troubled young girl just stood there breathing deeply, until she decided to get the screwed up letter from the drawer and let the housekeeper read it herself. "But my dear, you do want your mother to be happy, don't you?" Mrs. McGregor softly implored.

"But not this way, not yet," yelled Rosy. "It's too soon, she'll forget father."

"Your mother will never forget your father, Rosy, I am sure of that. Now come on, where is this gift, isn't that exciting!" Rosy glared at her.

"Effie, I'm not wearing it, mother's just trying to bribe me with that bracelet into liking this Simon man, and believe me, I most definitely do not like him." With that she fled fom the room and slammed the door.

So Rosy was having a very hard time, which was not helped by the fact that her uncle just would not cheer up. Evelyn dropped Rosy off at Ivy House after ballet one evening to be met by a terrible looking Tom.

He had hollow black circles beneath his eyes,

sickly looking skin and his breath smelt pungently of alcohol. He stared pitifully at Rosy, her family facial features a painful reminder of his deceased brother, and he heaved a great sigh before starting up the stairs without a word.

Evelyn glared at him and gestured that Rosy should go into the kitchen to find Mrs. McGregor, leaving her to talk to the man alone. "Tom," she began, her usually lyrically soft scottish tone becoming harder as she stared in disbelief at the man whom she loved when he was in a normal state. "Will you please tell me what's the matter?"

She received his glare without a flinch. "You know perfectly well what's the matter Evelyn, please leave me alone." Evelyn took a breath before breathing a quiet,

"No," then clearing her throat. "I mean, why are you still in this state after a month, Tom?" she implored.

"Are you trying to tell me how to feel, woman?" he snapped back, the first time he had ever raised his voice at her.

"I understand."

"No you do not," he cried. "No one does, my brother was very close to me."

Evelyn shook her head. "He was very close to Rosy too, he was her father." Tom sat heavily onto a stair.

"What has Rosy got to do with anything?"

Evelyn was astonished at the previously so generous Tom, now seeming so selfish in his own misery.

She understood, of course she did, she had been through a similar process when her mother had died not too long ago. But she also knew through her experiences what Rosy needed too, and that was a strong helping hand. Tom and his niece really needed to get through this dark period together, with the support of each other. At the moment the care involved was very one-sided.

"Rosy has a lot to do with everything!" she exclaimed, her voice rising to a loud, desperate cry as she tried to make him see sense for his own good. "Tom," she implored, quieter now, her voice catching in her throat.

"It it killing me to watch such a loving family fall apart. I am not even part of it, I just happen to be around you all of the time, helping with the café or dropping off Rosy and Audrey."

She paused to breathe and to see if her plea was having any effect on the broken man. "Please," she begged. "If only for my sake, move on. Your brother would want you to be happy, especially for the welfare of Rosy." She blinked back the tears that had began to trickle down her cheeks. "I just want my Tom back."

From where Tom sat on the staircase, the light that streamed from the stained glass window in the front door fell upon Evelyn making her mass of golden curls shine like a halo, framing her beautiful features as she tried to keep composed. He realised how selfish he had been, and that he had, without realising it, become disconnected from everyone around him.

He now understood that he needed to pull himself together in order for his beloved niece to be able to move on with her life as well.

He broke down in tears and a sympathetic but relieved Evelyn sat next to him on the staircase, rocking him backwards and forwards in an embrace until he calmed down.

Meanwhile, in the kitchen, Rosy and Mrs. McGregor had stood with their ears to the back of the wooden door, trying in vain to pick out sentences from the muffled conversation, wincing as the voices became raised and sharp and holding their breaths when it all went quiet.

Now deciding to risk it, they pushed open the door and crept gingerly into the hallway, a slightly confused Rosy clambering between the adults on the step and joining the hug.

"I don't know what we'd do without Evelyn, eh Rosy?" laughed Tom, smiling apologetically at his housekeeper, who nodded her appreciation, also relieved that he had finally seen sense.

"I'm sorry about everything," he murmered. "Will you forgive me?"

"Of course I will," smiled Rosy, content that what was past was past, and extremely happy to move on.

***

Life in the Lane household had greatly improved since Tom and Evelyn's little chat, and all were now going about their business much as normal. Of course, there was still much sorrow for Rosy and Tom, and Rosy still hadn't forgiven her mother for deciding to remarry so soon, but overall they were coping fine.

Two weeks later Tom dropped a bombshell: he and Evelyn were engaged! It didn't really come as a surprise to anyone as before the tragedy they were rarely seen apart, and they thrived off each other's sense of fun and humour. In light of the recent events, their relationship had taken a huge step forward, with Evelyn being the main source of emotional support for the family.

She would be moving into Ivy House after the wedding which was to take place the following May. Everyone was overjoyed, especially old Mrs. McGregor, who was delighted to have an extra helper for food preparations.

She had offered to teach her how to sew and make her own clothes, a growing neccessity as the wartime shortages required a heightened sense of 'make do and mend'.

The Price family were having dinner at Ivy House when the couple announced their engagement. Mr. Price choked on his potato, and Rosy and Audrey beamed at each other triumphantly. Tom held Evelyn's hand and reminded the party of the day when she had snapped him out of his depression.

"When Eve said all of these things I realised what a complete fool I had been. She was right. Me acting like a walking thunderstorm really wouldn't have helped Rosy get through this experience. What you need, Rosy, is a bit of warmth, a bit of spirit. And sometimes, being a man," (Evelyn rolled her eyes), "I am incapable of giving everything that a teenage girl needs. I realised that Eve was the perfect person for the job."

"So that's why you're marrying me?" the now slightly flustered Evelyn teased. She was really quite touched by Tom's moving speech. "You certainly love your niece," she smiled, putting her arm around an overjoyed, if slightly embarassed Rosy.

"Yes I do," he laughed. "But I love you just as much."

Chapter Seventeen
THE CHOICE

"**S**plendid! Another show, I can't wait," shrieked the pupils as they chatted in the changing rooms after an eventful ballet lesson with Madame Odette. The time had come again for the annual Christmas performance, however this year it was slightly different as the ballet school had been offered a theatre in a nearby town to present the show.

Of course everyone was extremely excited about it, especially Rosy, who had never actually performed in a proper theatre before. She was highly curious as to whether the experience was anything at all as Mr. Sayers, the drama school owner she had befriended recently, had told her.

She was also quite nervous. Madame Odette had told her that she was expected to audition en pointe for a role and she had only owned her shoes for a few months. But the competent teacher knew that Rosy had what it took to develop enough in such a short space of time to be in the running for a very good part.

"She has taken to pointe work like a duck to water!" she assured Tom one morning when she popped into his café for a quick cup of tea. "I have very high hopes for Rosy."

So it was with that confidence (passed on to Rosy through a very proud Tom) that the determined young girl entered the church hall one bright afternoon to audition for the lead role in the ballet, which was to be 'Romeo and Juliet'. Her prepared piece went smoothly without so much as a slip, and she landed the role of Juliet easily.

For the first few days of rehearsals it was a bit awkward as Audrey had fallen clean over in her audition and was lucky to have been given a part at all. Madame Odette, although very professional and strict, was also a kind soul and knew that Audrey could come up to scratch with no problem, giving her a substantial solo part to work on.

Rosy felt a bit embarrassed about getting the lead role twice in a row and knew that some people resented the fact. Still, she knew that that was what show business would be like and concentrated on learning her technically, and emotionally, advanced part.

When she had played Robin Hood the year before much less was expected of her acting performance. This time the role was an extremely heavy one and required strong acting ability, something that Mr. Sayers, who was still staying in the village, was happy to help Rosy with.

It came quite naturally to her and she found that

she enjoyed it immensely, coming home from rehearsals drained but satisfied. Her pointe work was coming on brilliantly, Rosy's diligent nightly practice taking her from strength to strength. The weeks flashed by and suddenly it was only three weeks until Christmas Day, and two until the opening night of the show.

At one rehearsal the principals were measured by Irene, Madame Odette's devoted assistant, who also happened to be very good with a sewing machine. She got to work immediately making the costumes, which Madame Odette had decided should be the best they had ever danced in.

The children didn't get to see their costumes, however, until the night before the show when they arrived at the theatre for the first time.

The auditorium was very smart, all red and gold and chandeliers, such a contrast from the dusty hall they usually performed in. Rosy was a bit disappointed that she didn't get her own private dressing room, being the leading lady. All the girls were in one room and the boys in another, but the cast was of less than twenty, and it was much more fun getting ready all together.

When they stepped out onto the stage for the first time the usually rowdy group became silent as they gazed out in awe at the rows of plush seats that surrounded them in a huge expanse of splendour.

There was a balcony and stalls, between them

amounting to about five hundred seats, with aisles leading down each side. The stage itself was complete with a wide array of lights and complicated looking sets of ropes suspended above the performers' heads.

The atmosphere was chilling. Even though there was no one in the audience an overwhelming presence could be felt, and the children hadn't experienced anything like it before. After a minute of dumbstruck staring the chatter began again.

"My goodness, it's like being a professional dancer already!" giggled Rosy, picturing herself taking her curtain call in front of such a large audience in only twenty four hours time.

They were instructed to go and apply full stage-makeup, of which more was needed now there were so many stage lights to be shining on them. This they did with much enthusiasm, knowing that it would not be long before their costumes would be revealed to them. It was a moment for which they had waited for weeks; they were 'quite spectacular' according to Madame Odette and Irene.

That moment came with many gasps of surprise and sighs of happiness. They were certainly fabulously made and in such expensive looking fabric, goodness knows where Irene had managed to get it all from in wartime. Jackets were studded with diamantes and bodices had lashings of ribbon and sequins. Everything felt amazing when worn.

Rosy, as Juliet, had a few costumes including a stunning powder blue velvet dress with slightly see-through chiffony sleeves, and another that was gold and sparkly with a very floaty skirt, worn for the romantic 'balcony scene' pas des deux.

As the dress rehearsal started, gramophone music swelled and the lights came up, dazzling the four boys that were on the stage at the time and making them lose concentration.

The rest of the cast jostled in the wings to catch a glimpse of this exciting new effect and all agreed that the lights put the finishing touch on the theatre experience and that they would never perform again without them.

That night Rosy tossed and turned, unable to get to sleep, her mind buzzing with snippets of music and sections of dances. She realised how big a responsibility she had as leading lady; she had to perform well to keep the show together.

The fact that the audience would consist of paying members of the public rather than the familiar faces of friends and relatives of the cast was a daunting one, and Rosy so wanted to make everyone proud by performing at her very best.

One scary thought was that the now rather well known to the family Mr. Sayers had decided to accompany Tom and Mrs. McGregor to the show. After all the acting tips he had given her, what if she forgot something and was a really unconvincing character?

It was lucky that Rosy fell asleep before she worried herself out of dancing at all.

***

"Wake up Juliet!" shouted Mrs. McGregor at eight o' clock the next morning, shuffling around the room making sure that Rosy had all her makeup, hair things, tights and ballet shoes packed in her bag ready to take to town shortly.

They were going hours early so that they could spend some time in the town, a novelty for the villagers. Mr. Sayers had said that he didn't mind that at all, he was just grateful for the lift and could easily find things to do for a couple of hours.

Rosy opened her eyes slowly, wincing as the rays of light that streamed through the south-facing windows fell straight upon her pillow. "What? What day is it?" she slurred, seeing her pointe shoes that were lying on her bedside table and remembering at once that it was the day of the opening of the show.

She got dressed as quickly as she could, losing a button and putting a finger through a stocking in her excitement. By midday they arrived in the town after a two hour drive, made longer than necessary by the slippery frost that had appeared overnight on the roads.

It was bitingly cold weather but Rosy didn't

mind as it gave her the opportunity to wear her smart fur-collared hand-me-down winter coat, having grown out of her old red one the year before.

The Price family met them by the fountain in the town centre, and after using up hours in the numerous shops it was soon time for Rosy to meet up with her friends at the theatre. Tom escorted her, glad to get away from the hoards of jostling Christmas shoppers, leaving the others to amuse themselves for the remaining two hours until curtain up.

They bumped into Fiona Craig a few streets away from the theatre. "Hello Rosy!" she grinned. "I bet you're excited, leading lady of a proper production in a real theatre!" Rosy jiggled up and down.

"Oh stop it Fi, you're making me go all goose-pimply again!"

They calmed themselves, making a good show of walking like respectable young ladies down the busy street, until they saw a giant poster in one of the shop windows. It read: 'Romeo and Juliet - week starting December 14th, proudly presented to you by the pupils of the Madame Odette School of Dancing, and starring Stewart Murdoch and Rosy Lane.'

The girls screamed in delight, too exhilarated to notice the looks of disgust they received from passers-by; their plan to keep cool and collected was almost forgotten. Bidding goodbye to their guardians they nonchalantly strutted through the stage door, and found most of the rest of the cast, boys and all, gathered in the girls' dressing room.

There they sat in a circle on the floor, discussing their excitement loudly until there was a sudden crackle and Madame Odette's husky voice began to speak from a very muted tannoy speaker in the corner of the room. When the announcement had finished one of the boys shouted, "Anyone actually catch any of that?"

"I think there was something about one hour to go and start getting ready now!" someone squealed. They all immediately jumped to their feet and launched themselves towards the sides of the room, each eager to get one of the six spaces that had a mirror. Rosy, in her excitement, got there first, saving a place for Audrey too. She beamed triumphantly as she began to lay out her assortment of belongings.

"Boys, get out of the room now, or I'll start getting undressed with you in here," announced Audrey, grinning at Rosy as the fun of the evening began.

The girls got to work smearing on thick greasepaint and pencilling their eyebrows until they were happy with the results, then they clambered carefully into their crisp costumes, impatiently waiting their turn to admire themselves in front of the single full length mirror.

Rosy sat at her mirror, which was framed by the traditional dressing room bulbs, and squirmed with happiness. She wished that she could bottle this feeling and experience it again and again at her leisure.

"Fifteen minutes!" came the next announcement, whereupon Rosy dashed out into the corridor to do some more vigorous warming up. It was at the call of "ten minutes" that her legs turned to jelly and her heartbeat increased to a scarily rapid pace.

Those last few minutes disappeared far too quickly, and, before they knew it, the children's nervous chatter was silenced by the final tannoy call of "Act One beginners to the stage please, you have five minutes."

Although she had only been in a show once, already she had grown to get a thrill from the expectant buzz of the audience, so she decided to find an out-of-the-way spot in the wings where she could wait and not get in the way.

She experienced, in utter bliss, the exhilarating moment when the house lights dimmed, the murmur stopped and the performers waited in the darkness of the wings, their hearts not beating until the music started and they found themselves carried away in the performance.

Juliet did not come on until the second scene,

so Rosy had plenty of time to psych herself up for her character; she was relieved to see her friends doing extremely well and looking as if they were enjoying themselves.

Her own performance went glitteringly, and she loved every minute. During the course of the ballet her character turned from a naïve young girl into a mature, passionate woman, and it was decided by everyone who watched the show during its four-night run that her acting was superb.

She came home flying high every night, longing to be back on that stage where she felt she truly belonged. On the final night of the show, Tom, Evelyn and Mr. Sayers came to watch again, and when Rosy took her curtain call, she was presented with a beautiful bouquet, labelled – 'To Juliet, with love from Tom and Eve xxx'. Now she felt like a real dancer!

As the clapping died down, Rosy waited for the curtain to fall, but nothing happened. Then she noticed Madame Odette striding confidently out into the spotlight, and holding out one of her hands for silence, the other hand clutching a microphone. "Ladies and gentlemen," she declared, her powerful stage presence still evident so many years on from her former dancing career.

"I 'ope you enjoyed the show tonight, but before you all go, I 'ave an award to present." An expectant hush fell over the audience and pupils.

"This will be only the second time I 'ave presented an award to one of my pupils following a show, and this time it goes to a young lady whom I am sure you will agree is exceptionally talented."

Rosy felt the pressure of hundreds of pairs of eyes on her and tried to look calm, even though she was bursting to find out who the prize was really for. As Madame Odette continued with her speech the tension built up inside Rosy. She was too nervous to believe that she was the winner, just in case she turned out not to be, but from what her teacher was saying, how could it not be?

"This girl 'as been with us for only just over a year, but from the first week she arrived at my ballet school I could see that she was a natural performer. She 'ad never been to a dance class in her life, but immediately settled in, making new friends easily due to her amiable and cheery nature.

"During the production of this show she 'as been an angel, 'elping out with the younger children and turning up to each rehearsal 'aving managed to perfect her performance overnight.

"This award is for her commitment, dedication, diligence and overall outstanding achievement. We 'ave never 'ad a leading lady quite like her. Well done to Miss Rosy Lane!" Rosy stood frozen in shock, the many diamantes that studded the bodice of her final costume glinting under the lights.

All she could manage to do was collect the

impressive looking trophy, curtsy her thanks and beam widely with pride.

All the way home Rosy talked with Mr. Sayers about the experience of being in the show while hugging the heavy trophy lovingly to her chest. "I think I am addicted to the theatre, is that possible?" The kindly old man laughed.

"I know for sure it is, in fact I know exactly how you feel." He sat in silence for a while, his brain working hard. "You know Rosy," he suggested. "From what I saw tonight, I think that you would make a truly brilliant actress." Rosy frowned.

"Thank you very much, but I want to be a ballet dancer."

"You are just the kind of person that our drama school would accept without a second thought. You definitely have acting talent there."

Rosy was plunged into confusion. "But this won't do, I want to be a ballerina, I have done for years."

She spent the rest of the journey staring out of the car window into the inky night, thinking about how much she had enjoyed acting the serious dramatic part of Juliet, accepting that maybe she loved to dance and act equally, and dreading the day when she would have to make a choice.

Chapter Eighteen
WEDDING DAY

Rosy sighed a long happy sigh as she twirled around Audrey's bedroom in her bright floral bridesmaid dress, the skirt floating up in a circle around her waist. "Oh Audrey, I've never been a bridesmaid before!" she sang. She loved the beautiful outfit that she had been provided with, and wished that she could look this stylish every day.

The two girls wore elegantly cut knee-length dresses in a light flowery fabric, fashioned from a pair of disused curtains. And they had somehow been found new silk stockings for the occasion, in which they felt exceedingly glamorous.

Mr. Price's sister had done their hair in neat plaits, and tucked sprigs of matching flowers into the pale blue ribbons that were tied in delicate bows at the sides of their heads, making the girls look like fairies out of picture books.

While the best friends were prancing around Audrey's room, Evelyn herself sat at her dressing table, staring blissfully at her reflection and applying her makeup as if in a dream.

Her aunt was breezily pinning sections of the bride's golden curls into a timeless up-do, chatting away about anything and everything, her airy nature managing to stop Evelyn from feeling too nervous.

Her bouquet of sweet peas from the garden sat in a vase of water on the windowsill, and an old white lace veil was draped over the back of the chair in the corner of the room. In fact Evelyn's entire outfit was antique; her mother had worn it for her own wedding twenty five years ago, and would have been very proud to see it being used again.

Luckily it was a warm but pleasantly breezy spring morning, perfect for the May Day wedding. Birds sang in the succulent boughs of the trees that lined the road from the farm to the church.

In the churchyard there were several frothy pink blossoming apple trees, a sprinkling of petals fluttering down like confetti with each breath of wind. There was not a cloud in the sky, and as the group walked excitedly down the gravel path to the picturesque stone building they could not have hoped for a better day.

Inside the church the ancient wooden pews were bursting with a large number of friends and relatives, each person dressed in their summer finery and laughing cheerily together, waiting for the bride to arrive at any minute.

The verger had taken great care over the presentation of the church. The brick-red floor tiles had been swept until they shone, and on each narrow windowsill was an abundance of spring flowers that looked beautiful against the bright whitewashed church interior.

Tom stood in his neatest, but still slightly threadbare, tweed suit at the front of the church. He smiled nervously at Mr. Price's brother, the best man, who handed him a flower to tuck into his button hole. "Good luck," he whispered, with a cheery pat on the back, as the guests hushed and Alistair the ballet pianist started to play the organ.

Every head turned to watch Evelyn shyly enter, arm-in-arm with her father and followed by a grinning Rosy and Audrey. Their dainty white leather court shoes clicked in time with the music on the tiles.

The bride looked spectacular. In these times of make-do-and-mend she had done a very good job of taking in her mother's white wedding dress to fit her own slim figure, and had spruced it up with a blue satin ribbon retrieved from one of Audrey's old ballet costumes and tied in a large bow around Evelyn's waist.

The dress itself was made of a lightweight milky-white fabric with an overlay of lace that came right up to her neck. It swished pleasingly as Evelyn walked down the aisle, a modest train sweeping along the floor behind her, joined by the veil which rippled from a headdress of flowers to the floor.

She caught Tom's gaze and smiled radiantly, handing her bouquet to Audrey, who sat with Rosy on the front pew to watch the service. Gradually, as Evelyn and Tom knelt in front of the altar, the sun came round and flooded through the stunning stained glass window, radiating coloured light upon the couple and creating a picture beautiful to behold.

As they were pronounced man and wife, Mrs. McGregor burst into tears and everyone cheered for minutes; there had not been a wedding in the village for years, making this day an even more momentous occasion.

The guests filed out into the churchyard, everyone admiring the gently swaying irises that nestled in the vivid green grass and the patches of turf that were entirely carpeted with snowy white daisies.

The richly flowering apple trees cast long, cool shadows over the appreciative guests as they waited for Mrs. McGregor and other helpers to make sure that Ivy Café was ready for the reception.

Before long, word reached them that everything was sorted, and everyone started out on the leisurely walk along the beach to the venue.

"Congratulations, Mrs. Lane!" giggled Audrey, catching up with her sister who was tiptoeing across the sand with her skirt hitched up for fear of ruining her precious dress.

"Mrs. Lane sounds like my mother," snorted Rosy, reminded for a second of the troublesome marriage that was soon to take place back in London.

All unhappy thoughts flew away when she saw what the imaginative housekeeper had done to the café. A painted banner had been strung across the front of the building, saying 'Just married – congratulations Tom and Evelyn!', and pretty little vases of primroses had been placed on each table.

There were just enough tables to seat everyone, and they all enjoyed a low-budget wartime buffet of tinned salmon sandwiches, scones and small cakes.

Most of the guests were too poor to buy wedding presents, and there was nowhere nearby to purchase them anyway, but they were more than happy to bring food and drink. Mr. Morrison brought homemade apple cider, and old Mrs. Ferguson came along with a sack of nuts from the trees in her garden.

The two families had saved up their ration coupons in order to buy enough flour and sugar to make a small tiered wedding cake. The cows of Allaway Farm provided sufficient milk for this purpose, and also to make cheeses and cream to accompany the locally picked berries preserved from the previous autumn.

"Where's the haggis?" shouted one loud local, everyone laughing as Evelyn grimaced and clutched her stomach in disgust. "Come on Eve, you're a Scot born and bred, it's in your genes to like haggis," teased Tom, grabbing her round the waist, picking her up and spinning her round in a circle.

"Oh do stop, you annoying man, I will not have that revolting stuff anywhere near my wedding!"

There were, however, hazelnuts from the trees opposite the beach and Mrs. McGregor had made a deep basin of trifle, adding a good deal of whisky to the dish as Rosy found out when she swallowed a large spoonful and burnt her throat! The villagers had not seen such a spread since before the war, and when every last scrap had been gladly consumed the guests sat extremely full and content.

As the sun turned a vibrant amber and began to sink towards the horizon, Mr. Price made a brief speech about the antics of Evelyn as a small child. He had every person in fits of laughter and turned the bride's cheeks to crimson.

Next Tom stood up and thanked everybody for coming in the usual manner. This was followed by some entertainment from the same men who had played for the Christmas Ceilidh, and then the tables were cleared to the side for dancing.

Before the celebrations finished for the evening and people were about to start the long walks back to their cottages, Tom tapped a glass with a spoon to gain attention and lovingly took his new wife's hand. "I just wanted everyone to know how incredibly grateful I am for meeting Eve," he said.

"As I am sure most of you appreciate, I, and Rosy here, recently suffered a great loss, and without Evelyn I would be a broken man still. In her love for this family she helped us to get our lives back on track. Without her I don't know where we would be."

Mr. Price chortled, "Well you wouldn't be here at all, laddy!"

"Oh yes," Tom nodded. "And she might have saved my life once as well!" With that the party dispersed, and at about one o'clock in the morning, after helping to clear up the café, Rosy went back to Ivy House with Mrs. McGregor and reluctantly took off her finery.

As a wedding present from a family friend of Evelyn, the newlyweds had been lent a quaint stone cottage in a neighbouring village where they drove, straight after the reception, for their honeymoon. Travelling further afield was out of the question in the country's current circumstances, not that they minded. They loved Scotland, it had brought them together and was where they were sure they would spend the rest of their days.

Everyone involved in the wedding came away happy and optimistic about the future. Rosy lay in bed that night wondering about what her own life would bring, whether she would meet someone as nice as her uncle to marry, where she would live, and what career she would have.

This brought her back to the obsession she was continually struggling with, and she fell asleep still trying to work out her true ambition.

Chapter Nineteen
UNEXPECTED NEWS

Ivy House had never been a happier place since Evelyn moved in. The only person who was not ecstatic with this development was Audrey who was now left lonely at Allaway Farm. As her father was a busy farmer she was left to herself for much of the time. She made up for this by being with Rosy whenever she could.

She practically lived at Ivy House, eating dinner there more often than not. Luckily, Mr. Price did not mind. He was glad that his younger daughter was able to go somewhere and be among friends and relatives when he was unable to look after her himself so often, and he occasionally joined the family for meals. They were all, of course, delighted when he did.

In fact, Rosy and Audrey spent so much of their time together that they often forgot that they were not sisters, finding great amusement in reminding everyone that Audrey was indeed a kind of half-aunt to Rosy.

The change of circumstances that Tom and Evelyn's wedding had brought about had not however changed life much in the small Scottish village. If anything it had made life more enjoyable.

On the other hand, in dark, war-ruined London, Rosy's mother had proceeded to marry her American Air Force pilot and then had moved to America with him, much to Rosy's deep distress. Just before the wedding she had written to Rosy telling her she was saving to buy her some tickets for a real ballet, and would send them when she could manage it.

To be honest Rosy would have been more than happy to forget all about her previous city life. She would never forget her father, but after her mother had moved on so quickly it was hard to accept the reality.

She just concentrated on making the most of her village life which she had grown to adore over the few years that she had spent in Scotland. As a result, her life continued to be as rich and colourful as it would have been if these few hardships had not have existed.

***

A year after becoming Mrs. Lane and a few weeks before Rosy's fifteenth birthday, Evelyn was invited to take part in a biannual national riding competition that was taking place near the village.

They decided to make a day trip out of it. Mrs. McGregor made a picnic lunch of bread, cheese and apples, and packed a large glass bottle of lemonade as a treat.

The horsebox was to be pulled by Mr. Price's big old Austin 14, and consequently the journey was going to be a long one, not that anyone minded.

The villagers were used to living out in the sticks and travelling long distances to get to anywhere at all. This made car journeys an opportunity to have a good singsong, something that the Lane family enjoyed throwing themselves into whenever possible.

At the last minute before departure the hamper was flung in the back of the car, where it filled up most of the foot room meaning that Audrey and Rosy had to travel the hour-long journey with their knees up near their chins.

Mr. Price sadly had to stay at home to tend to his fields, so Tom drove while Mrs. McGregor and Evelyn somehow managed to squeeze into the front with him. Off they set, merrily singing at the tops of their voices and brandishing the paper flags they had made to wave during the competition.

When they arrived they were all a bit stiff, but nevertheless in high spirits about the event. "Are you coming girls?" bellowed the housekeeper, struggling with an array of flags, blankets and parasols. "Eve needs time to get her horse ready you know."

"Hang on a minute!" shouted Rosy. "Can you

just extract this hamper so we can try to unfold ourselves?"

A steadily more nervous Evelyn disappeared with her precious palomino mare, Vera, to change and warm up, while the others eventually escaped from the car and set up camp on the grass verge where the public were to sit to watch. After all the kit had been unpacked it looked as though the four enthusiastic spectators had brought enough stuff for them to camp on the spot for a week.

They had clashing tartan blankets to sit on and large parasols to protect them from the burning rays of the sun. They had also erected a banner which said 'Good luck Eve!' in bold red letters and they waved their flags with great gusto.

Looking round it seemed to them that they were the only ones who had made an effort. Everyone else seemed to be rich equestrian types in hacking jackets and highly polished riding boots. They turned up their noses at the rowdy group who had decided to have as much fun as possible and nothing less.

"Oh dear, this seems a bit like Ascot," chortled Tom. "Oh well, we'll teach these posh snobs how to have a good time!" At first the teenagers had felt rather embarrassed about the behaviour of their party, but before long they had got into the spirit of the competition, cheering raucously whenever a rider cleared a jump or executed an impressive dressage manoeuvre.

Soon it was time for Evelyn to compete. Her class was cross-country, and her supporters watched in awe as the tall jumps and wide water troughs were set out ready for the trials to begin.

Soon Evelyn trotted timidly into the arena. Audrey burst into laughter as she saw her sister kitted out in a full riding outfit of hacking jacket, red and navy stripy tie and a hair net.

"Oh dear, I'm used to seeing her in blouses and skirts, isn't the whole thing just so pretentious?" She received a hard elbow in the side from Rosy as several disapproving heads turned and glared angrily.

"I think she looks very smart," said Rosy, "At least she's the only competitor who's managed to look glamorous at the same time. Rather unconventional competing look with the red lips..." The competition committee could make her dress up in a hairnet, but no one was going to deny Evelyn her lipstick.

All the young woman's anxiety disappeared as she spotted her colourful fan club sticking out like a sore thumb from the rows of 'respectable' spectators, and she tried not to laugh.

She found it hard to concentrate with Tom, Mrs. McGregor, Rosy and Audrey all waving their flags and shouting her name, but she was a competent enough rider to soar over the obstacles with ease, coming first in her first round.

She did not expect, however, to make it through to the final, and was exhausted by the time she cleared her last fence, coming a respectable fifth place much to the delight of the others. They pounced on her as soon as she had tended to her horse and came over to them.

Audrey gave a knowing look at Rosy before mimicking their ballet teacher's strong French accent. "'Ave you done your glute stretches Eve? You don't want your thighs to become tight and bulky!"

"Wow, Eve, you're the fifth best horsewoman in the nation!" cried Rosy, joining Audrey in hugging the fatigued Evelyn earnestly.

"Give the poor woman some space," fussed Mrs. McGregor, prodding the girls with the end of her walking stick. "She looks positively faint."

"Thank you, Effie," stammered Evelyn, shakily loosening her tie. "I do feel rather dizzy." At that, she collapsed in a dead faint into a panicked Tom's arms, coming round some minutes later with the help of an event marshal.

As soon as she opened her eyes, she was bombarded by questions from Tom who was worried sick. "Are you ill? Is it shock? Can you stand?" he pressed, confused as his wife shook her head and grinned.

"I'm absolutely fine, Tom, really," she laughed

softly, touched at the fraught man's care for her wellbeing.

"No you are not fine," he gasped. "You've just been unconscious for a while."

"I'm fine, I shouldn't really have ridden today, but it's perfectly normal," she soothed, sitting up and thanking the marshal, who, satisfied with seeing her upright and smiling, hurried off to direct the traffic from the showground.

"I was going to wait until Rosy's birthday to tell everyone my news then, as a sort of present, but it looks like you want an explanation now, doesn't it?"

Mrs. McGregor cottoned on first, raising her eyebrows in disbelief and nudging the girls as it dawned on them too. Tom's jaw dropped almost to the ground, and he snatched up Evelyn's hand. "You're not, are you?" She nodded, gleefully, and hugged him. He couldn't speak all the way home.

At eight o' clock they arrived back at the village, dragging Evelyn's overjoyed father away from the fields to enlighten him with the news. He abandoned his tractor to join them at Ivy House for a celebratory meal, which was great fun, especially as Tom kept going into dazes and having to be snapped out of them by an amused Rosy.

Audrey was invited to stay overnight in Rosy's room, and they stayed up long past midnight having intellectual conversations covering life, death, politics, childcare, religion, the war, their future lives and of course the new baby. They were sure they were the only two best friends in the world who lay in the dark at one in the morning philosophising, but they enjoyed it.

"I wonder if I'll have any children when I'm older," whispered Audrey. "I'd like to."

"So would I," sighed Rosy, dreamily. "Well you won't be able to if you're a ballet dancer," reminded Audrey. These harsh words hurt Rosy, but she knew it was the truth. She would have to sacrifice her dream of raising a large family in order to follow her other dream of being a dancer, but on the other hand, if she became an actress, it would be possible for her to have children at some point.

She shared this revelation with her shocked friend, who had no idea that Rosy was even considering any other career but ballet. Audrey thought that Rosy's new acting idea was just a whim that had come from her recent overwhelming success in Romeo and Juliet, so just agreed, relieved that her own chosen career of nursing wasn't as complicated as show business.

Chapter Twenty
DISASTER STRIKES

Taking a deep breath, Rosy carefully wrestled out the stiff dressing table drawer and laid it on her bed, slowly slipping a dog-eared brown envelope out from beneath the now discarded silver locket.

Opening the package, she took out the two ballet tickets that her mother had posted to her some weeks ago. After much deliberation she had decided to put aside her anger about her mother's speedy remarriage, go to the ballet and take advantage of this rare opportunity.

When the tickets arrived Evelyn had offered to accompany Rosy to the theatre for the occasion, even though she was then seven months pregnant. Having lived in the Highlands all her life she had never been able to see a real live ballet, apart from, of course, Madame Odette's annual dance school shows.

They were going to stay overnight in a hotel and spend the next morning exploring the city, much to their excitement. In fact, Rosy and Evelyn had begun to count down the days to their outing. Until then Rosy had a few weeks in which to occupy herself, and, much to her dismay, Audrey had gone with her father to visit his sister in Glasgow. They were due to come back the day of the ballet trip, but after Rosy and Evelyn would have left the village.

While strolling in profound boredom one day through the tent-less campsite, Rosy was overjoyed to bump into her old friend the drama school man Mr. Sayers. He was laden with bags and on his way to Ivy House where he would be spending his Christmas holiday, this time with his family.

"Are you still dancing?" was his first question, followed by, "And have you played in any more high dramas recently?" He chuckled, turning to his equally stout and jolly wife.

"Muriel, this is the little ballet dancer I was telling you about," he twinkled. "The one who I noticed for her raw acting talent." Rosy stood, embarrassed, on the grass, suddenly preoccupied with rolling a stone around with the sole of her shoe. "Actually Rosy, I spoke to my directors at the drama school; they are very keen to meet you."

Rosy gulped, "Meet me? Really?" she stammered, flattered that Mr. Sayers thought her talent worthy enough of publicising.

"Have I told you I think you have potential?"

"Yes," Rosy breathed. "Once or twice." Her face reddened as she became quite het-up under the pressure. "Everybody keeps telling me to become professional in different fields, it's really confusing me."

She was just about to politely excuse herself from the situation and go away to think, when she heard a breezy, "Hello!" from behind her. She froze, immediately wishing she had not blushed so violently.

She turned and saw a friendly smiling face staring straight at her. It belonged to a young, good-looking boy of about sixteen, with laughing bright blue eyes and a well-built figure. Rosy swooned.

"Rosy, this is my son Robert, he's staying with us for the week this year," said Mr. Sayers. "Now why don't you two go off and get acquainted?"

Rosy readily agreed, and from that day on made firm friends with Robert, glad that she had found someone to talk to while Audrey was away. On their second day together she took him on the same tour of the village that her uncle had given her over three years ago when she had first been evacuated.

Neither of the pair had siblings and they both loved to perform more than anything else, so maybe it was these similarities that brought them so close together. But it was on this stroll through the picturesquely snowy village when Rosy learnt that Robert had just, this September, enrolled at his father's drama school.

Immediately the questions flowed from her

lips, and the friendly boy was more than happy to satisfy Rosy's curiosity about everything from boarding to lessons.

She was intrigued by the thought of moving back to central London to spend her whole time studying the performing arts and was thrilled to learn that all the drama students also learnt a wide variety of dance styles, although, sadly, ballet was not one of them. "So are you going to audition next March then?" he asked.

"No, my ballet teacher is arranging for me to audition for the Sadler's Wells Ballet School," came the excited reply. "That's where I'm headed."

They stood in silence for a long minute, watching the glittering flakes of snow spiral gently down to the ground and settling to form a blanket of powdery whiteness that coated everything in sight, making the bay eerily silent.

Rosy sighed, shutting her eyes and letting the snowflakes settle refreshingly on her eyelashes. "Are you sure you want to be a ballet dancer?" said Robert, staring intensely at Rosy, only breaking his gaze to blink away the biting snowflakes as they flurried into his face.

"Yes," nodded Rosy, crumpling as she gazed into her new friend's imploring eyes. "Yes... no." Her worries came pouring out to Robert, who listened patiently and attentively. "From the age of nine I have worked myself to tears to follow my dream of becoming a ballet dancer," she wailed, her throat becoming choked as her emotions rose to an unbearable level.

"I still want to dance, but part of me is having doubts. I don't know, it's just been really stressful lately. My ballet teacher says that if I am truly serious about ballet I need to audition for the Ballet School this February."

She threw her hands to her forehead in realisation. "My word! That's two months away!" Calming herself down, she linked arms with Robert and they continued to stroll along the now completely white strip of grass that bordered the sand.

Shrugging noncommittally she began to speak again, the friends striding in step as they reached the end of the beach then clambered up the bank onto the contrasting hardness of the compacted and frozen dirt track. "I know I want to perform, I just don't know whether I want to specialise so harshly just yet." She sighed, her spirits rising once again as she remembered that Robert was to have dinner with them at Ivy House that evening.

"Anyway, that's enough of my troubles," she smiled. "I'll race you to the fence!" By the time the two arrived panting at the icicled fence around Ivy Campsite Rosy had forgotten her worries and was back to her usual, vivacious self.

She enjoyed the evening greatly, warmed by

both the roaring fire in the kitchen grate and the general exuberant atmosphere of everyone who sat squeezed round the small table.

A few days later, the Lane family bade a sad farewell to the Sayers, and the few remaining chilly winter evenings leading up to Rosy and Evelyn's long awaited trip to the ballet seemed to drag on terribly. Rosy found that she was beginning to miss the friendly and supportive Robert, and couldn't wait to tell her best friend about him when she arrived back.

Rosy and Evelyn spent the evening before the trip listening to Vera Lynn, Evelyn's favourite singer, on the wireless, while preparing their outfits for the morning. Evelyn hummed along to the cheerful tunes sweetly but slightly less tunefully than Vera, dancing as enthusiastically as she could with her exceedingly large bump.

Rosy reread the letter which had arrived from Audrey that morning, longing for her to be coming to the show as well. Audrey was jealous of her best friend and big sister's ballet tickets. She wished she could go too, but would just have to be content with Rosy's follow-up report, which would no doubt be so detailed, and so speedily and eagerly recounted that it would be practically incomprehensible!

Rosy managed to finish her sewing by ten o'clock, at which point she went straight to bed. She did not want to be too tired to enjoy the ballet, especially as an early rise was in order to catch the early train.

She woke at seven o'clock the next morning and hurried to dress herself, taking extra care over her appearance seeing that she would be mixing with rich, bejewelled ladies at the theatre and didn't want to make a fool of herself. She had left London a dishevelled, scruffy evacuee, and was planning to appear at the ballet looking like the proper young lady she now truly was.

Making a last-minute decision she took the discarded silver locket and placed it once more around her neck, its familiar weight resting against the rose-pink velvet of her dress. She also retrieved the beaded bracelet she had been sent over a year before and let it sparkle proudly on her wrist. Her mother had saved up for the tickets after all.

She checked the wall clock and scurried down the stairs, panicking that the early train would depart without them. There were only two trains to Inverness a day, the first at nine o'clock and the second at two.

After catching the train from the village station, they would change at Inverness, and make a similar tiring journey down the country to the one that Rosy had made when she was evacuated so long ago.

As she burst through the door to the kitchen she expected to find the usual morning scene of Tom reading his weekly newspaper, Mrs. McGregor bustling about preparing breakfast and Evelyn sipping her first cup of tea. (Apart from Vera Lynn, tea was Evelyn's other love. It was not unusual for her to drink six cups in a day.)

Instead, Rosy found an empty house. The usual whistle of the kettle and rustle of newspaper pages were replaced by an unnerving silence.

She searched the house from top to bottom, calling out in vain, and she was about to run out of the door to find help when she glimpsed a piece of white paper on the table top in the kitchen.

She hadn't noticed it before in her shock but now gingerly picked it up and scanned it quickly. The writing was scrawled, and had obviously been written in a hurry.

It was in Mrs. McGregor's instantly recognisable copperplate hand, and explained briefly: 'Have had to take Eve to hospital in Inverness, the baby's coming. Please stay at home until the Prices get home from Glasgow, and I am sorry about the ballet. I don't know how long we will be.'

The first thought that came into Rosy's head was a selfish one. "I'll never get to the ballet now," she thought in alarm, before coming to her senses and realising the true seriousness of the situation. Evelyn's baby wasn't due for nearly a month; she hoped nothing was seriously wrong.

She hurriedly wrote her own note, which she

left next to Mrs. McGregor's on the kitchen table, then she snatched her coat from its hook in the hallway and hurtled out of the door.

Panic rose inside her as she sprinted away from the lonely house and, while she ran, she wondered whatever could have happened.

The road was icy and in her haste Rosy almost slipped over several times, cursing loudly as she skidded towards Allaway Farm like a drunken ice skater. When she arrived at the farmhouse she clenched her fists and hammered desperately on the door until her hands were sore both from the impact and from the cold. There was no reply.

"Audrey," she sighed, "I need you, why aren't you home yet? It's well past nine already and I've missed my train." Her plaintive cries turned to sobs of worry and disappointment. She had been looking forward to seeing the ballet for so long, and didn't know if she would ever see another one again. Her family had gone and taken the car with them, and she seemed all alone in the village.

She sunk down on the frozen stone doorstep, not noticing the biting frost that coated everything, or the winter wind that had begun to howl spookily through the trees. A goose honked, a twig snapped, and still no sign of Mr. Price's battered old motor car.

Rosy sat silently, waiting, worrying, for at least an hour, before really feeling the gusts of icy air and pulling her coat more tightly around her.

She realised that it was no use waiting any longer, and, remembering what happened to her uncle the last time he was outside in harsh weather conditions, she decided to make her way back to Ivy House.

Wiping away a tear she stood up slowly, thinking that she would have been on the train to the ballet by now. But there was no use in crying. It was too late. The train had gone.

However, one thought played on the deflated girl's mind. There was still one train to Inverness, at two o'clock. If she could somehow get there in time she could still see the ballet. She had the tickets safe in the pocket of her dress, but there was no way that she would be able to walk to the train station. It was over five miles away and at this time of year she would freeze to death before she got there.

Suddenly a thought hit her: She could ride to the station, she just had time. She had to get to see the ballet somehow, and Tom, Evelyn and Mrs. McGregor would certainly be at the hospital for a while. She didn't even stop to think of the consequences of her actions.

She knew that although she hadn't ridden for over a year she was still a competent rider and could safely manage the short journey, even with the harsh weather conditions. At least it wasn't snowing.

Chapter Twenty One
A CHOICE MADE

Rosy wound her gloved fingers into the grey pony's thick mane and clung on as they trotted cautiously along the glassy road that lead to the train station. Normally, Rosy would have stopped to marvel at the unearthly spectacle of the frosted hedgerows. Each tiny leaf had turned to silver with a furry layer of crystal-like ice, but now she had bigger things to think about.

She wondered if she was doing the right thing. Was it insensitive to disappear to enjoy herself at a show, knowing that one of her most loved friends was in hospital, and not knowing the seriousness of the matter?

"They would want me to be happy Nessie, I know that," she muttered, forgetting her 'mature' decision to stop talking to the horses as she used to do at the young age of twelve.

"Eve would understand, she knows how much this trip means to me." She lapsed into silence, the rhythmic thuds of Nessie's hooves on the frozen dirt track becoming quite meditative to her, reminding her of the happy days she used to spend riding the beautiful grey horse for hours on end when her only worries in life were the outcome of the war, bad dance technique and homesickness.

"I do hope Eve is alright," she sighed, before noticing a humming sound in the distance, and pulling Nessie to a skiddy stop. It was a low flying aeroplane. In a matter of seconds, the imposing four-engined aircraft was directly above the girl and horse, flying very low and fast, suddenly casting an enormous dark shadow to join with its deafening, animal-like roar.

Nessie snorted in terror, rearing suddenly onto her shaking hind legs, her panicked bulging eyes rolling frantically in their sockets. The next thing Rosy knew, the side of her body came brutally into contact with a sharp wooden fence, and then the ground. The poor horse had galloped madly back towards the village for some unsuspecting passerby to encounter.

Pain seared through Rosy's body making her black out for a few seconds in a lightheaded faint. When she looked down at her left leg she screamed a long, horror-stricken scream, a ghastly, upsetting sound that floated across the silent countryside, lingering hauntingly in the crisp air.

Blood seeped from a deep gash in her upper thigh, creeping through the ice and turning it to a bright crimson.

Rosy felt nauseated by the sight, and when she tried to move she sent a blinding shock of pain into her leg which shot through her body to her head, causing another brief period of light-headedness. In intense pain she managed to haul herself up beneath a sparsely leafed evergreen tree which offered some protection from the cold, damp ground.

There she waited, sobbing through a mixture of pain, regret and resentment, for what seemed like hours.

Unknown to Rosy, following the incident, the Prices had returned from their stay in Glasgow and were of course highly alarmed to find their fully tacked-up pony hurtling down the road towards the car. Mr. Price tended to the shocked animal, while Audrey let herself into Ivy House, found the two notes, and at once realised what had happened.

She knew her best friend too well and immediately got her father to begin driving to the train station, knowing that something must have happened to Rosy along the way.

They were not two minutes into the journey, when Audrey spotted the vivid patch of blood and nearly passed out herself. She then saw a dark shape slumped under the tree. "Rosy!" she screamed, jumping from the car in an instant, not caring about the dangerous road condition as she slipped and slid towards her best friend.

"Audrey, thank goodness," came the weak reply from Rosy, who had managed to keep herself from freezing to death by rubbing her numb body with her hands, and continuing to move through the pain. She could feel, apart from the obvious impressive gash, that there was something badly wrong with her upper leg.

With each movement the bones almost screamed out and she knew that she was doing increasing damage to her injury. However, she also knew of the possible effects of hypothermia which could take hold if she remained immobile.

Mr. Price took her as quickly as he could on the long journey to the hospital where an efficient nurse gave her some drugs, and Rosy slipped away into a stress-free sleep.

Audrey and her father made sure she was alright and then crossed to the other side of the small building to see to Eve and Tom, who were still having trouble in the maternity ward.

***

A sharp stab of pain woke Rosy, who opened her eyes to find herself in a neat little room with a single window and a wilting vase of flowers on a table next to the bed on which she was lying.

Hours had past, and it was now about seven, the time that Rosy and Evelyn would have been entering the theatre for the ballet. Rosy felt a pang of sadness as she saw the time from the clock on the wall and registered this disheartening fact.

A smartly dressed nurse bustled in shortly after and smiled kindly at Rosy, before asking her all manner of questions about how she was feeling. She was told that she had a deep visible wound and a fractured femur.

The first thought in Rosy's mind at that moment was towards her dancing, something that she was forced to think about minutes after she had woken up and found herself unable to move her legs without excruciating pain.

"Rosy, your uncle will be coming to see you just as soon as his wife's had the baby," smiled the nurse upon leaving the room. "Oh, but there seems to be someone to see you now," she added in surprise.

Rosy strained to hear who it was and picked up a very strong French accent mixing with the young nurse's high pitched, Scottish intonation.

"Madame Odette," groaned Rosy. She was not at all ungrateful for her ballet teacher's effort to make the long journey to see her, but was not really in the mood to be lectured about her potential, something that often happened in meetings with her.

In came the flamboyantly dressed Madame Odette, bringing with her a handmade get-well-soon card and an overpowering smell of exotic perfume.

From the moment that the woman walked in Rosy could sense that something was wrong. The cheeky sparkle had faded somewhat from those dark expressive eyes that were so similar to Rosy's, and her cheery smile seemed somehow forced.

"I'm sorry the ballet plan didn't 'appen," she began, sitting stiffly at the end of the bed. Rosy nodded, unable to sit up to greet her visitor because of the restricting plaster casts that had appeared overnight on various parts of her body.

"God obviously doesn't like the idea of me seeing the ballet," the patient sighed, staring at her lap to avoid her ballet teacher's sympathetic gaze.

"It looks like God doesn't like the idea of ballet at all Rosy," murmured Madame Odette. Rosy looked up, unnerved by this sudden statement.

"What do you mean?" she stammered.

"The first thing I did when I arrived was to talk to the nurses about your injury," came the soft reply. "You 'ave a compound fracture which will take months to heal. I didn't want to be the first person to tell you this," she faltered, pausing as Rosy held her breath in panic.

"My dear, you will certainly miss the audition, and I'm afraid that you may never be a professional dancer now."

For Rosy, the world had just ended. She never expected to hear this. She just lay there with her eyes shut while she tried to swallow the news, before breaking down into devastated tears.

"I've been so stupid," she cried. "Why did I try to ride to the station, just to see a silly little ballet?

And now I've ruined everything!"

"You 'aven't ruined everything, Rosy," said Madame Odette, cradling the sobbing teenager in her arms.

"I've let you down," Rosy choked.

"No you 'aven't," soothed Madame Odette. "You could 'ave been great, but that's in the past now and I'm proud to 'ave taught you."

Rosy took a few minutes to get over the shock then just sobbed incredulously while the now slightly awkward ballet teacher sat there in thought. "And at least ballet isn't your only talent," she smiled. "I 'ave heard from a certain Mr. Sayers that you have everything needed to go to his drama school."

"I have been worrying about what to do with my life for months," whispered Rosy with a rapidly beating heart. "It looks like that decision has been made for me, doesn't it?" She tried to smile confidently back at Madame Odette, who gave her a warm hug and began to leave the room.

Rosy knew that her ballet teacher was right. At least she had another road open to her, one that she knew, if she was successful, would still provide a rich and wonderfully fulfilled life.

"Oh là là!" exclaimed Madame Odette, who was halfway through the door. "It's like Piccadilly Circus in this corridor!" Rosy wondered who on earth it was to see her this time, but all became clear

198

when Tom, Mrs. McGregor, Mr. Price and Audrey came one after another into the room. It was quite a squeeze. Then Rosy noticed a tiny, wriggling bundle in her uncle's arms, and forgot all about her own tragedy.

"Oh!" she squealed, beckoning frantically to Tom to bring the baby over to her so she could get a real look at it.

"Rosy, meet Daphne Lane," beamed Tom, obviously bursting with pride as he cradled his daughter lovingly in his arms. She was beautiful. She had bright blue eyes like her father's and a few fine fluffs of hair curled onto her forehead and around her face, framing her adorable features which were dainty and elflike just like Evelyn's.

"Eve sends her love," he continued, then frowned uncomfortably. "And her sympathy. We really are truly sorry about your dancing." Rosy squirmed with pleasure as Daphne curled her miniature hand around her little finger and refused to let go.

"Don't worry about it, it's fine." She smiled, much to everyone's confusion. They were expecting to find a devastated, broken young girl, but instead Rosy now seemed to be coping.

There was no point crying over spilt milk, Rosy decided. She had learnt that over the years. After seeing Tom and Evelyn's new baby, she had realised that there were so many wonderful things in the world to be happy about, and she now needed to concentrate on what she *had* got, instead of worrying about things that were past.

Of course she was devastated about not being able to be a ballet dancer, but she knew that she had other talents for which she was very grateful. She told all this to the relieved and overjoyed gathering, who crowded around her bed to hug and kiss their brave Rosy.

"Yes, thanks Rosy," grinned Audrey. "Now I'm the best in the ballet class at last!" Daphne then began to cry softly, giving cute little gurgles intermittently.

"It looks as though someone's suffering from lack of attention," laughed Tom, who said his goodbyes to his niece and left the room, followed by a dazed Mr. Price who was still in a state of shock after becoming a grandfather.

Rosy and Audrey smiled at each other, and old Mrs. McGregor, predicting a long, loud and giggly conversation between the best friends, promptly left to find a cup of tea. "I can't believe we've all ended up in hospital together," began Audrey.

"Well at least I got to see little Daphne straight away," Rosy said, grabbing her friend's hand in excitement. "You're an aunt now, Audrey!" she chortled. "I do wish I could hold her."

"You can, as soon as you're well enough."

"You know, I think it's fate that I fell from that

horse," murmured Rosy. "Maybe I was meant to be an actress." Audrey digested this new piece of information, and smiled.

"Well at least you don't have to make that difficult choice anymore!" They lapsed into silence as they contemplated the day's events, at which point Mrs. McGregor re-entered and stood holding her steaming mug of tea, amazed.

"Silence?! That's novel," she exclaimed.

"We're fifteen now Effie," Rosy reminded her, rolling her eyes. "We're not small children!"

"Although we may act like it sometimes," added Audrey, pirouetting and knocking the vase of dried up flowers from the bedside table. It fell to the floor, surprisingly staying in one piece but leaving petals strewn everywhere.

She received a glare from Mrs. McGregor, and grimaced. "Well, they were nearly dead anyway," she squeaked, and decided to make a quick exit.

Rosy leaned back on her pillows, exhausted from her emotional afternoon. She smiled bravely at Mrs. McGregor, who twinkled back and picked up the fallen vase with the hook end of her walking stick. Rosy was glad her life was full of such wonderful people.

Chapter Twenty Two
A NEW JOURNEY

A few years later came the end of the war, and with it came the time that Rosy had to leave Scotland and embark on a journey back to London to start her training as an actress.

Rosy had left hospital after what seemed an eternity of lying flat on her back, and had returned to ballet classes two years later in order to very gently regain the strength in her legs. She turned up only for the gentle barre-work warm-ups at first, but gradually increased her time as she built in strength and stamina.

A beautiful coincidence meant that the day she managed her full class since the accident, the war was declared over and there was even more cause for celebration!

The day after this good news, Rosy awoke to find that the sky had turned an unusually intense blue for the time of year. The cruel flurries of snow the region had suffered over winter had long been gone. She had worked hard to regain her strength and balance with the same determination that had been so apparent in her over the years.

She was proudly able to join Tom, Evelyn,

Mrs. McGregor, Audrey, and of course her beautiful little cousin Daphne, to attend a magnificent street party in order to celebrate the end of the horror that had been the Second World War.

Evelyn skipped down the road holding her daughter, who giggled with glee, grabbing at her mother's thick flowing hair. Tom followed, watching euphorically and smiling to himself.

The others walked slowly and sauntered along behind as Rosy was still slightly weak from her injury and grew tired easily. Mrs. McGregor was now even more old and creaky so she couldn't move fast anyway, and Audrey was more than happy to drag along with them.

"Keep going grandma!" she teased, and Mrs. McGregor hit Audrey playfully with her walking stick. "I wasn't talking about you, Effie!" grinned the leggy eighteen year old, "I was talking to old Rosy here."

Rosy snorted, having become used to jokes about the slow speed of her walking. It wasn't that she couldn't walk any faster, it was just that she didn't have the confidence to speed up yet. However, at Audrey's remark, she briefly broke into a run to chase her friend.

Laughing ecstatically, she ran a few more paces and grabbed onto Audrey's arm in shock. "Audrey, I ran!" she screamed, self-belief flooding back as she realised that her life was almost back to normal.

"Goodness gracious Rosy, you're not an invalid!" gasped Audrey, forgetting about Mrs. McGregor with her huffing and puffing, and pulling Rosy along to catch up with Tom and Evelyn.

"You managed a whole ballet class yesterday, for goodness sake! Even if you didn't do all the steps it's still a great achievement. You've been able to run and things for ages, you just didn't have the confidence to try." Audrey giggled. "Imagine *you* not having confidence," she added. "Miss Drama School 1945!"

"You mean Miss Bighead 1945!" shouted the breathless housekeeper from several yards behind them. As the best friends waited for her, Rosy couldn't stop grinning. She remembered that she would be starting Mr. Sayers' drama school after the summer break.

She was to be one step closer to finding her feet on the professional stage and didn't know how she was going to be able to wait. Mrs. McGregor caught up with them and they walked the last few minutes of the journey in contented silence.

They arrived at the busy street where they found a carnival-like atmosphere with flags and colourful bunting strung from the cottages, and all the village people gathered ready to celebrate.

The distinct lack of men was still noticeable, but would not be for much longer as the surviving soldiers would be returning from their fighting over the next weeks.

A line of tables taken from the cottages stretched along the road, decked with an abundance of sandwiches and cakes. The village children were already seated, laughing excitedly and waving paper flags.

Rosy and Audrey took seats next to the Morrison twins, who had recently shot up in height and towered over everyone else. There was no need for their trademark coloured hair ribbons anymore; Edine had cut her stunning fiery red hair into the latest fashionable permed bob so it was now easy to tell the two apart.

As the party began, Mr. Morrison brought from his house a gramophone which blasted out cheery songs, adding to the joyous atmosphere of the street. Tom and Mrs. McGregor rushed back and forth from Ivy Café with pots of hot tea for the adults, and afterwards there were numerous party games for the younger children. Rosy and Audrey joined in, but soon gave up, giggling after being beaten at most of the games by five year olds.

As the sun set across the sparkling bay everyone sang 'God save the King' before dispersing back to their homes in different parts of the village, leaving the clearing up to be done next morning.

Rosy cried, knowing that it was the last time she would ever be with all the villagers around her, having fun and laughing into the night. In a week's time she would leave on the train for London, and might not be coming back to see the people who she had grown to love deeply, for years.

***

"Of course, when you've made your fortune as a world famous film star, you won't forget your old uncle will you?" joked Tom at the platform, his jovial outside appearance hiding what was really an intense sorrow at saying goodbye to his niece after six years of looking after her as if she were his own daughter.

Rosy was already settled on the train, having said the majority of her goodbyes the night before. Mrs. McGregor, Madame Odette, Tom, Eve and Audrey were the only people left to bid farewell to, and as they stood in a solemn row on the platform, Rosy knew that it was to these close friends that saying goodbye would be the most difficult.

She hardly knew where to begin. She leaned out of the window, relishing the Highland breeze which was singing in her ears and blowing tendrils of hair across her face.

"I want to thank you for everything you've done for me, all of you. I have learnt so much from my stay here and I can honestly say that it has been the best time of my life. How I can ever thank you for your kindness I don't know, but I promise I'll come back and visit just as soon as I can!" Beaming smiles mixed with tears as the billowing steam of the engine began to fill the platform.

"I can't believe it," sighed Madame Odette. "Little Rosy off to drama school! I knew something wonderful would 'appen to such a delightful performer. It matters not what discipline you do, but I thank my lucky stars that the unfortunate accident with the 'orse did not end up robbing the stage of Rosy Lane."

"Oh stop it, do, you'll reduce me to a blubbering mess!" blushed Rosy, leaning further from the train window to give her ballet mistress a hug. "I can't tell you how excited I am about drama school. I don't think the next few days until term begins will be able to pass quickly enough! It's funny - I thought I had a tricky decision choosing between acting and dancing. It so happens that falling from the horse that Christmas made the choice for me."

She smiled. "It looks like it will be the right one after all!" And with that, the train began to creep from the station and Rosy once more pressed up against the window to wave, not stopping until they pulled round a bend and out of sight.

An anxious Evelyn slid her trembling hand into her husband's and dabbed at her eyes with a handkerchief. She was frightened at the concept of

Rosy having to re-adapt back to the bright lights and bustle of London from life in such a tiny sheltered Scottish village. "She will be alright won't she?" she murmured, shakily.

"What, our Rosy?" smiled Tom. "Of course she will..!"

THE END

8124458R00119

Printed in Great Britain
by Amazon.co.uk, Ltd.,
Marston Gate.